THE POLE DANCER

Another Julia Lillus Crime Thriller

JAMES ROBERTS

Edited by
JAMES ROBERTS
Illustrated by
JAMES ROBERTS

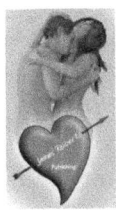

Cover Design Copyright © 2020 James Roberts

Cover Art Copyright © 2020 James Roberts

Illustrations Copyright © 2020 James Roberts

ISBN: 978-1-7361234-6-1

Library of Congress Control Number: 2020923098

Published by James Roberts Publishing

Printed in the United States of America

This book is a work of fiction. Names, characters, businesses, places, events, and incidents are either the products of the author's imagination or used in a fictitious manner. Any resemblance to actual persons, living or dead, or actual events is purely coincidental.

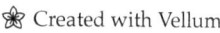 Created with Vellum

CONTENTS

Introduction   v
Preface   vii

1. THE WITCHES   1
2. SEX TRAFFICKING   3
3. THE PLAN   5
4. ANGELA   9
5. THE HIT   11
6. THE INDUCTION   14
7. RICHARD   18
8. THE SWEARING IN OF CLOTHING   19
9. SENSITIVE CONVERSATION   22
10. THE SWEARING IN OF MAKEUP   23
11. THE SWEARING IN OF DANCING   24
12. COMPLETION OF INDUCTION   26
13. RICHARD AND THE OTHER PATRON   28
14. THE BAR CONVERSATION   30
15. ANOTHER CONVERSATION WITH A PATRON   33
16. THE HIGH BIDDER   35
17. WE LOST HER   39
18. HUGO WARNS CHUCK   42
19. JULIA GOES ABROAD   44
20. JULIA LANDS IN SAUDI   47
21. AT THE SHIPPING DOCK   49
22. THE TAXI RIDE   51
23. THE DISCOVERY   53
24. JULIA'S PLAN   55
25. THE LESBIAN SKIT   60
26. THE ESCAPE   63
27. THE SHIPPING DOCKS   65
28. THE SHIP   68
29. THE HUNT FOR THE GIRLS   70
30. THE CAPTAIN   72
31. HOT COALS   75
32. THE FIRE   78

33. THE LANDING 80

34. WELCOME HELP 82

35. BACK AT THE OFFICE 84

36. ISLAND ATTIRE 85

37. NO SEX TONIGHT 87

38. THE ESCAPE PLAN 90

39. BOARDED 92

40. THE CALL 94

41. TOSSING COOKIES 96

42. RICHARD IS NOT INCLUDED 97

43. BOBBIE IS HORNY 98

44. THE STORM 99

45. MORNING 101

46. THE HIDING 104

47. POOR YOUNG GIRLS 109

48. THE PANTIES 111

49. NEW YORK 113

50. THE FBI 115

51. BOBBIE EXPLAINS 117

52. SOMEONE IS IN MY HOUSE 118

53. THE CONFRONTATION 120

54. THE ASSAULT 124

55. BACK AT THE OFFICE 130

56. THE PROPOSAL 132

57. THE PACKAGE 134

About the Author 137

INTRODUCTION

This book is a work of fiction and continues alongside the Julia Lillus Series of Crime Thrillers by James Roberts.

"I feel like I have absolutely nothing on. This top is so low it barely covers my dark...."

"It is just fine. As long as you don't show them, you will be fine. The top is tight enough, so your nipples won't peek out."

"I feel like I am falling out of these bottoms in the crotch area."

PREFACE

Sex trafficking has become the number one crime in the United States and abroad. This book gives insight on how it can quickly come about, how an undercover female is purposely entered into one crime ring and the dangers of vulnerability.

Julia Lillus and her Department enter into a secret, but a dangerous scheme to shut down the ring, to where she, herself, is put directly into the danger of exploitation.

Chapter One

THE WITCHES

"Good morning Amanda, Richard, and Bobbie. How are you all this morning?" asks Julia.

"Uh oh, when you call us all into your office, Julia, we know something is up and another bizarre case like the one over in the Poconos," says Richard.

"Richard, I heard a little bit about that."

"Yeah, Julia. It was most bizarre. Some kind of a witch coven…"

"A witch coven?" asks Amanda.

"Yeah, at a resort. Supposedly some guy was visiting the resort and became obsessed with a witch, although he didn't know she was a witch at the time. During the time of his stay, all of the other witches there were 'serviced' by him."

"Richard, 'serviced'?" asks Bobbie.

"Yeah, Bobbie, much of what you do for me…."

"OK, Richard, you can stop there. What happened?" asks Julia.

"Well, one of the witches killed him in such a bizarre manner. You know, like the Hobbit case years ago."

"Oh, Richard, that is disgusting!" exclaims Amanda.

"The whole resort burned to the ground, and the story ended like that in Shakespeare's' Romeo and Juliet. The guy was buried up on a hill, and his witch lover threw herself upon his grave and burned up in a fire. All that was left was a charred corpse. At least that is the rumor. No one knows for sure."

"Geesh Richard, are you glad we didn't have to respond to that one? " asks Julia.

"I am glad we hadn't. I would not have wanted to subject Richard to those witches. No telling what kind of trouble he would have gotten himself into."

"I don't know Bobbie. It might have been quite the experience….," says Richard.

Chapter Two

SEX TRAFFICKING

"**O**K, guys, here is what we have on our plate today. I have learned there appears to be an underage trafficking scheme in the works," states Julia.

"Is this a sex trafficking case?" asks Bobbie.

"My hunch would be, yes," answers Julia.

"Where is this being played out?" asks Richard.

"The information I received is a place called 'The Poles'," answers Julia.

"Oh, I have heard of that place. It is over in Clay County. It is a big pole dancing establishment. I heard there is non-stop pole dancing with twenty poles simultaneously," says Richard.

"And you know this how Richard?"

"Well, Bobbie, it is big talk among the male population around here as you might have guessed."

"You haven't been there, Richard?" asks Bobbie.

"Oh no, I wouldn't dare!"

"You got that right, mister," Bobbie remarks sternly.

"You would think underage girls would be easy to spot," says Amanda.

"Well, I have heard they are not easy to spot because they have some sort of scheme in making those girls look older than they are. You know nowadays how the younger females are so much more developed," says Julia.

"What are the ages we are talking about, Julia?"

"Thirteen, fourteen up to sixteen, Richard."

"Such a disgrace," says Bobbie.

"The entire pole dancing routine is running an undercover auction for those girls. Certain patrons go there to watch those girls perform and bid on them. The girls are sold to the highest bidder," says Julia.

Chapter Three

THE PLAN

"So, how do we penetrate the scheme?" asks Bobbie.

"Richard, you being the only male in our Department, will become one of the so-called 'shoppers," says Julia.

"Oh no, here we go again!" exclaims Bobbie.

"Don't worry Bobbie, Richard will only be bidding on one of us, and he will bid high enough to not allow any sale except with his bid," states Julia.

"OK then, which one of us is the pole dancer?" asks Bobbie.

"Unfortunately, ladies, we are much too old for that role. They can't make us look like teenagers," says Julia.

"Aw shucks, Julia, I would have liked to see one of you ladies pole dancing."

"I bet you would, Richard," says Julia.

"Richard, will you behave yourself? So, who will be the pole dancer?" asks Bobbie.

"Amanda, would you like to answer that?" asks Julia.

"The pole dancer will be my sister. She is almost like a twin sister and looks younger than she is. She is nineteen and looks much like me."

"Wow, watching your sister pole dance, and she looks just like you? What an assignment I have!" exclaims Richard.

"Richard, please remember you are married and a father to three adorable girls," says Amanda.

"Yes, I know, I was just kidding. Bobbie, I was just kidding. You know you are my 'pole dancer'," says Richard.

"She will have to go through the induction process. She will need to convince them she is fifteen years old. I am sure she will be inducted. She is a drama student in college, and she has loads of experience acting and looking like a younger teenager," says Julia.

"What if the induction process involves, well, you know, sex?" asks Bobbie.

"My resource assured me there is no sex involved with those girls when they are on auction. Once they are sold to the highest bidder, well, who knows what would transpire then," says Julia.

"You do know, Richard, your part in this stops at the sale?"

"Bobbie, who do you think I am?"

"Let's not answer that," says Julia.

"I am a bit concerned about what may happen if, by some chance, Richard loses the bid for my sister. I don't want to subject her to such a dilemma," says Amanda.

"That is a risk, Amanda, of which we have to be certain won't happen. We will have a secondary plan in place if such a thing did happen, but we won't let it happen. I will be sure Richard has enough money so that no one can outbid him," says Julia.

"So, what are we to learn from this?" asks Bobbie.

"We will learn about the induction process. How they obtain those young girls and who is at the top of this scheme. We will also learn about the patrons doing the bidding. Those guys will lead us to the actual trafficking market," answers Julia.

"Once I purchase Amanda's sister…"

"Richard, her name is Angela," replies Amanda.

"OK, so what happens to Angela once she is purchased?"

"We are not sure, Richard. You will have to find out. But she will become your property, so you will need to be sure you claim her as fast as you can so that nothing happens to her that we don't want," says Julia.

"Julia, what does your resource say about how much my sister, the girls, have to undress during their pole dance routine?" asks Amanda.

"I am told, once again, the girls have to be 'clean' during auction before the sales. That means no nudity and no sex. They will undoubtedly have to dress in skimpy and provocative clothing to show off their 'wares' for prospective buyers. He said the outfits he has seen during the dances involve a 'G-string' type bottom with no pubic hair showing and a top showing plenty of cleavage but no nipples."

"This is going to be a very delicate 'sting'," states Bobbie.

"Yes, Bobbie, very delicate, and that is why we will all wear radios so we can communicate with each other. Now Richard, once you complete the purchase of Angela, I want you to as quickly as possible take her home to Amanda's house."

"Sure, no problem with that Julia. What will I use for the purchase?"

"To be sure you will win the purchase of her, the city is giving us six hundred thousand in large bills. Hopefully, you will not need that much, but we need to be safer than sorry. You cannot fail with this, Richard. You must bid high enough for the purchase of Angela," states Julia.

"Amanda, you will need to give Richard a change of clothes for Angela. She will need to cover up as soon as possible. We cannot let her back to the dressing room to pick up the clothes she wore to the establishment," says Julia.

"Bobbie, I want you to be at the bar overseeing the operation and keeping a keen ear to all conversations. A soon as you see Richard and Angela leaving, I want you to convene here at the office to work on tying the loose ends," says Julia.

"Julia, how dangerous will this be for Angela? How can we be sure she will be accepted for inclusion?"

"Amanda, you and I, along with Angela, will go over all of that tonight. It can be dangerous, but we are going to plant a 'bug' on Angela so we can hear all of the conversations and be alerted if she appears to be in danger. Don't you worry. If there is any danger for her whatsoever, 'sting' or no 'sting,' I will intervene. I will be right outside the establishment in an unmarked car."

"Thanks, Julia. Angela is my only sister, and I sure as hell do not want any harm to come to her."

"As far as the inclusion in the establishment, I believe it will not be a problem. Your sister is a beautiful woman, and there is no way anyone would not want her to be part of an auction where she can draw huge money. Richard, before you drop Angela at Amanda's home, make sure you get all extraneous information from her we were not able to hear on her 'bug'. She will have to remove and hide it as soon as your bid becomes the winning bid, because I assume there will be very close contact with many people during the processing of your payment and the release of her," says Julia.

"How are we going to orchestrate the 'sting' Julia?"

"Bobbie, we will figure that out when we convene. There are too many loose ends right now. The first thing we need is to get Angela into the auction ring and then safely get her out. Richard, please follow Amanda to her home and be ready to take Angela to the bookstore, which is one block from the 'Poles' establishment."

"OK, I am on it, Julia."

Chapter Four

ANGELA

"Hello, Angela. My name is Officer Richard Peltz, and I am going to be your partner throughout this operation. May I ask why I am dropping you off at the bookstore?"

"Bookstores are Internet hotspots, and a lot of teens hang out in those establishments. I feel the bookstore would be a good place for possible young girl pickups."

"I see. So, let's go over what you will be doing. Once you are at the bookstore, you need to be on the lookout for any men entering. I don't have to tell you to be provocative but make some kind of gestures that would entice a visit with you."

"Officer Peltz, is this enticing enough?"

"Yes, showing some thigh with a short skirt will be enticing enough. Now, be sure to play along with the gentleman and don't give him too much all at once. We want to hear the procedure for luring young girls."

"I won't have a problem with that."

"Once you get into the establishment, be sure you are out of harm's way. Both Julia and I will be close if you need us. Julia said her resource guaranteed you would not have to dance nude or enter into any sexual activity. As you know, I am going to be the highest bidder and purchase you. Be sure to hide the 'bug' as soon as the bid is final. I would suggest putting it somewhere that is out of reach, such as in your bra, because you will not have many clothes on at that time. You are not to show you know me or give any indication you are OK with me purchasing you. I will have to act like I just purchased a piece of 'meat'. I hope you don't mind if I put my arm around your waist as I lead you out to my car. I will have to give gestures of wanting to touch you in private areas of your body, but I won't. It has to look real to them. Those patrons are just animals, and they tend to have their way with the girls before they get them ready for the streets or whore houses."

"Mr. Peltz, I trust you. Do whatever you need to get the job done. I will not take it personally," states Angela.

Chapter Five
THE HIT

"Hey darling, I hope you don't mind if I have a seat here, at the table?"

"Yeah, I guess it will be all right. It is a free country."

"I couldn't help to see your well-toned legs."

"Listen, mister! If you are here to try and pick me up, it isn't going to happen."

"No, no, that is not why I am here. I was just complimenting you. So, what brings you to the bookstore?"

"I come here often to catch up on assignments for my school."

"Oh, what school do you attend?"

"Gentry High School."

"Yeah, that is just a couple of blocks away. I am guessing a sophomore?"

"Yup, I have just two more years."

"And then what? What are you studying?"

"I want to be a photographer."

"That is a great field. What photos are you hoping to concentrate on?"

"I think modeling, glamour, lingerie, and maybe some nude."

"Look, I am glad I met you here. I think I might have a way for you to practice your photography skills and at the same time, earn some extra cash."

"What do you have in mind?"

"What if I were to get you into an establishment where you can practice your skills and use those photos for your school projects? It would be a great opportunity for experience."

"OK, so what is the catch? I am sure there is something I will need to do to get paid."

"How about dancing? Can you dance?"

"Dancing?"

"Yes, you will have the opportunity to photograph the dance models, and at the same time have fun dancing yourself."

"Oh, so you want to get me into a dance club? No way, I am not that kind of female. Besides, I am only fifteen years old. Don't you have to be eighteen to work and dance in a night club?"

"You are thinking of a strip club, which this is not. You will definitely pass for an older girl."

"So, it isn't legal for a girl of fifteen to dance in a club?"

"Look, you will have the opportunity to make quite a bit of money each night dancing. One hundred dollars a dance, say ten dances, you could easily bring a thousand cash a night. That is why I was complimenting your leg tone. I know you can easily make that kind of money."

"There is one thing. What will I be wearing or not wearing if I were to take you up on this offer?"

"Nothing less than a two-piece bathing suit."

"I don't think I want to dance in my bathing suit in front of mostly men."

"Listen, all they do is watch. They are not allowed to touch you or make any erotic gestures toward you. Look, right here is an advance on your first night…one thousand dollars cash. If you are willing to start tonight, I will throw in another five hundred dollars. So, what do you say? You get the opportunity to be the photographer you want to be and make a huge amount of money just parading around in your bathing suit like you would on a public beach."

"You say no nudity and no sex in any way?"

"Absolutely! I promise this establishment is not a typical strip club."

"Well, a thousand a night can go a long way towards my college tuition. By the way, why me? Did you plan this meeting?"

"No, you see, I am a recruiter for this establishment. They are always looking for dancers because dancers come and go at will. By the way, I did not catch your name. My name is Tim."

"I am Angela. Nice to meet you, Tim."

"So, Angela, what do you say? Are you ready to start? Do you want fifteen hundred dollars cash right here and now?"

"Well, hmmm…"

"Look, show up at the establishment called 'The Poles' on Broadway, just a few blocks from here."

"'The Poles'? That is a pole dance club."

"Yes, but not like you think. Can I depend upon meeting you there tonight at around 7 pm?"

"OK, I think so."

"Look, once you learn more about the position tonight, you can decide if it is or isn't for you. There will be no hard feelings. I will see you at 7 pm tonight."

OK, Tim."

Remember Angela. I can assure you no striping, nudity, or sex.

OK, Tim, I will take your word on it.

Chapter Six

THE INDUCTION

"Yes, Amanda, this is Julia."

"Angela got the offer to the 'Poles'. She is going there tonight to get her induction."

"Did she say how it went?" asks Julia.

"She said the guy is a smooth talker and knows how to lure young girls with flattery and sweet talk. He works on the emotions and dangles a carrot of big dollars in front of their noses. He promised a thousand a night dancing."

"Wow, that is very interesting. It means the auction block must be running with a high rate of revenue," states Julia.

"Hello, Angela. I am glad you decided to come to work for us."

"I can back out if I don't like what I hear?"

"Certainly, Angela, I stand by my word. Come in. I am going to introduce you to the manager, and she will give you all the information you need," says Tim.

"OK, thank you Tim. Will I see you again, Tim?"

"Oh yeah, now and then."

"Here is Angela. Angela, this is Patricia. She will be your 'go-to' person for all your needs and questions. You will be in good hands with her," says Tim.

"Angela, how old are you?"

"I am fifteen and a sophomore at the Gentry High School, Mrs....."

"You can call me Patty or Pat. It doesn't matter. Did Tim give you all the details to what you will be doing here at this establishment?"

"Yes, he did."

"I was told you were studying to become a photographer and want to hone your skills, photographing some of the dancers and submitting your work for school projects?"

"Yes."

"No problem," says Patricia.

"I believe I will be a pole dancer?" asks Angela.

"Yes, at first. You will be shown by our senior girls how it is done. I assume you are familiar with strip club dancers; you have heard of them?"

"Yes, and I told Tim I wanted nothing to do with that."

"Don't worry, Angela. Our dance club is different. None of our dance routines involve stripping. We don't allow our girls to wear anything less than a two-piece bathing suit. You can't show any pubic hair or nipples. There is no nudity."

"I have no problem with that," says Angela.

"You are not allowed to approach our patrons for any tips, and they are not allowed to offer tips in the usual strip club manner by placing them in your top or bottoms. We do not condone tipping in any manner—one more important point. There is to be no partaking of sexual acts of either gender, male or female, who are patrons, dancers, or staff. There are no private dance rooms at our establishment. So, you see, we aren't a strip club," states Patricia.

"But how do the patrons, men, get their jollies at this establishment if they cannot touch but only watch? Don't they look forward to private dance rooms and placing tips on the dancers' bodies? Isn't that what they pay for?" asks Angela.

"Our patrons are not of that type. They are much more

sophisticated and professional. We have never received a complaint from them wanting more."

"That is very strange. I can't believe men can watch and be satisfied without getting off somehow."

"Angela, you do not to worry what they do with themselves watching the dancers. The point is they are not allowed to touch any of the girls while dancing or otherwise. They do vote on who they feel are the best dancers. The girls who have the most votes gets a bonus in their pay. The bonus is their tip to you. You can easily make a grand a night if you are a good dancer."

"I am assuming that grand is over and above the one hundred dollars a dance?" asks Angela.

"Oh, yes, the one hundred a dance is guaranteed. The establishment pays that to you. I will warn you, though. We have twenty girls dancing simultaneously, and it is very competitive. The better you dance, the more dance opportunities you will have and the more tip bonuses you will receive."

"How does one compete?" asks Angela.

"As I said, we do not allow striping nude, but you will have to dance very provocatively. Our gentlemen want a good 'rise' out of watching the dancers if you know what I mean."

"Yes, I understand, but I am only fifteen. How do I dance provocatively?"

"Our senior girls will teach you, and I know my dear, just in being a female, I am sure you have some idea how to be provocative?"

"Well, I guess I do. It is tits and ass," says Angela.

"Yup. You get out there and wiggle your ass and shake your tits while sliding your crotch up and down the pole!"

"Well, if you want to put it that way. Will I get time to photograph the dancers?"

"Yes, Angela, but you will want to dance to get the most money and the tip bonuses, won't you?"

"Yes, I need to save money for my college tuition. Is this legal for me at fifteen years of age to be doing this?"

"Angela, you won't be nude, and besides, you will not look fifteen when we get done with your make-up. My senior girls will take care of that. We have never had issues with the ages of the girls we hire. As long as there is no nudity and no sex, the authorities leave us alone. If you have more questions, I can address them later, but I want to get you over to the girls to get you trained up and ready to dance by the end of the week."

Chapter Seven

RICHARD

"OK, I can see their mode of operation with the induction process. They are pretty clever, I would say," states Julia.

"Yes, and they don't let on what the so-called 'voting' entails," remarks Bobbie.

"Angela was very good at asking those questions. I don't think they suspected anything. She sure doesn't look fifteen," says Richard.

"Richard, I hope you related to Angela, where to place the microphone 'bug' so that it can't be seen or fall off of her," states Julia.

"I did, and she decided to place it in her bra securely."

"Richard, I hope you didn't assist her in placing the 'bug'?"

"Bobbie, my sweet, how dare you to ask me a question such as that! But, if you ever need to wear a microphone 'bug', I can assist you in placing it."

"I am sure you will, Richard," states Bobbie.

"Ok, guys, do we need a timeout here? I can go sort files while you two love birds take a break," says Julia.

"Julia, you wouldn't happen to have a spare 'bug' I can borrow?"

"Richard!" exclaims Bobbie.

Chapter Eight

THE SWEARING IN OF CLOTHING

"*L*adies, this is Angela, our newest recruit. I will leave her with you. She is to be performing at the end of the week," says Patricia.

"OK, Patti, we will have her ready."

"Angela, my name is Kate, and her name is Kim. I will take care of clothing, make-up, and so on, while Kim will teach you the dance."

"How old are you, Angela?" asks Kate.

"I am fifteen years old."

"My, you are a well-developed girl for your age. I won't need to fix you up too much."

"Fix me up?"

"Yes, Angela, I need to make you look older than fifteen."

"Why don't they just hire older girls?"

"They tried that, and the patrons felt the girls were too old. They wanted a fourteen or fifteen-year-old dancer for their pleasure. We give them that, except make them look a little older. You see, the business survives on the likes of the patrons and their money to come and watch, but they don't want to be seen gawking at 'children'. We have to oblige, or the establishment goes under. Pretty warped, huh?"

"Yes, men, your patrons, want to have sexual fantasies with underage girls. That is sick!"

"True Angela, but men will be men, and we have a business to run," says Kate.

"Disgusting!" exclaims Angela.

"Angela, are you still with us? Do you want to continue?"

"Yes, I guess so. I just hate the idea of what the patrons will think of me and the sick fantasies they will have."

"Remember, Angela. It is a business. You will harden to it."

"OK," says Angela.

"Good, now go over there and change into these, but first put the top on and place these in each cup covering your nipples."

"Why, what are these for?" asks Angela.

"They are to add a little padding giving you a larger cup size, and we cannot have the nips showing erect out on the dance floor. It can be cold at times when the air conditioning is blasting."

"Wow! These clothes or whatever you call them are quite dazzling with all the sequins attached. The bottoms look a little revealing," says Angela.

"Go ahead and put them on. We will adjust the bottoms as needed."

"Wow, Angela, you look amazing! That outfit certainly reveals the beautiful woman you are. Your toning is just excellent. I can imagine the tip bonuses you will get."

"I feel like I have absolutely nothing on. This top is so low it barely covers my dark…," states Angela.

"It is just fine. As long as you don't show them, you will be fine. The top is tight enough, so your nipples won't peek out."

"I feel like I am falling out of these bottoms in the crotch area."

"You will get used to it. Hmm, yup, I believe the amount of padding in your top will do," says Kate.

"I am afraid it will fall out while I am dancing."

"Nope, they won't. Now, for your bottoms, you need to shave your pubes. You cannot have any hair down there poking out of your bottoms."

"Do I need to shave down there? Can't I just bleach it?" asks Angela.

"Nope, no pubic hair can be seen."

"Tim mentioned I would wear a bathing suit. I would never wear this on the beach or even in public. I feel so much like a whore! My ass cheeks are as bare as can be, and this insufficient material running up my crotch from behind…How can I be sure my pussy won't show?" asks Angela.

"It won't. This drawstring is your friend. It will tighten things up down there just by tugging at it. Now, let's take a look at the make-up portion of your readiness. You will need some mascara, lip gloss, and eye shadow," says Kate.

Chapter Nine

SENSITIVE CONVERSATION

"Richard, I was caught off guard. I didn't want you to have to listen to all of that dialogue. I will be sure not to tell Amanda you heard the sensitive nature of the conversation," says Julia.

"I was OK with it, Julia."

"I am sure you were, Richard. Please go file some paperwork. We will call you if there is further important dialogue, but not of a sensitive nature," says Bobbie.

Chapter Ten

THE SWEARING IN OF MAKEUP

"**G**reat Angela, you look stunning with just the correct amount of mascara and eyeliner. The crimson lip gloss brightens your face. How do you like the midnight blue eye shadow?"

"Kate, I must say I like it a lot. How do I get this as perfect as you have gotten it every time I dance?" asks Angela.

"That's why we are here. I will do your makeup before each dance. You will look stunning out there for the patrons," says Kate.

"Kate, are you sure I don't look like a whore? I feel like one as I gaze at my entire body in this mirror."

"No, no, no! You mustn't feel that way. Remember, we are not engaging in whore activity. None of the girls are showing their bare tits and asses to the patrons. Now, I will take you over to Kim."

Chapter Eleven

THE SWEARING IN OF DANCING

"Angela, you look stunning! First things first, have you ever shaved your pubic hair?" asks Kim.

"No….I," says Angela.

"Well, you might feel a little prickly down there, and because you will be doing a lot of sliding on the pole mainly with your crotch, I want you to apply this salve between dances. It will help with the prickly feeling. Have you ever pole danced before, Angela?" asks Kim.

"No, I have never even thought about it."

"OK, the important thing to remember is to keep the pole on your crotch at all times. That will be your pivot point ninety percent of the time. There will be times when the pole is nestled between your breasts. You need to be sure that is where the pole lands. The last thing you want is to get a tit squished between the pole and you, to put it bluntly. Watch me. When you lift your legs such as this, be sure to push your ass out and give some wiggle to it. You are going to want to let your tits bounce as well. Look. Watch me. There are six moves in the dance routine, and when you have completed move six, you will start all over and repeat them. Any extra moves you want to do just may land you with more tip bonuses. Just remember, you must move provocatively at all times during your performance. Your gage as to whether you are moving provocatively enough will be the gaze in the patron's eyes. You will detect their approval or disapproval. Now, grab onto the pole and watch me. I want you to mimic my moves. After we are finished, I want you to spend the rest of the evening practicing. You will need to have these six moves down by the end of the week."

"I guess I am doing this, OK. What does it look like to you, Kim?"

"Angela, do you have a boyfriend?"

"Well, not at the moment…"

"What if you have a boyfriend at this moment, and he is asking to have sex with you."

"Wait a minute…"

"Hang on, Angela. Hear me out. First off, would you like to have sex with him?"

"I guess so…well, yes."

"Of course, you would. What female doesn't want it? OK, so what will your boyfriend need from you to get 'laid'?"

"I guess I need to get him aroused."

"Exactly! How will you get him aroused enough to be able to have sex with you?"

"I would need to remove my clothes and systematically…."

"Yes, that is correct, and don't you think you need to show some tits and ass with some physical moves which cannot help but to beg him to screw you? Am I correct?"

"Yes, I believe so."

"That my dear is the provocativeness you need to display while dancing."

"Wait a minute, Kim. You said no nudity, so no tits and ass and no sex!"

"Correct! You show tits and ass through your outfit. You don't show them nude. You are not having sex with them, but you do need to arouse them enough to make them feel like they need to 'bed' you right away as you are dancing."

"I don't know if I can live with myself thinking I am turning the patrons on in that manner," says Angela.

"Fifteen hundred plus bucks, my dear, each night! Just saying."

Chapter Twelve

COMPLETION OF INDUCTION

"Julia, those women are whores in disguise."

"It appears that way, Amanda."

"I feel sorry for my sister. She isn't very familiar with sex and nudity. I don't mean she doesn't know anything about those things. My sister and I were brought up to be proper young ladies, and I assume Angela is feeling very uneasy at the moment."

"I am sorry we have to subject her to this, but us old gals couldn't do the part."

"I think that you two could have pulled it off," says Bobbie.

"OK, it sounds as if Angela's orientation and induction are complete, and she is going to be spending some time practicing. Richard, the auction starts Friday night at seven sharp. You need to be there then. I don't think they have an order to which girls are up to auction first. We cannot afford any slip-ups. God help us if she were to be won by another patron."

"Don't worry, Julia. I will be there right on time."

"OK, now we wait until showtime Friday night," says Julia.

"Angela, have you gotten the six dance moves down?"

"Yes, Kim, I am ready for tonight."

"You will dance for approximately twenty minutes at a time. There is a billboard on the dance floor with the names of the dancers who are performing. When your name disappears off of the billboard, you are to leave the dance floor and return to the dressing rooms. Use that time to freshen up. The dressing rooms also have a billboard showing the girls currently dancing, and when your name shows you are to return to the dance floor and find a vacant space to start your routine. Remember, twenty girls are dancing at one time, so it is hectic. You will fit in just nicely. That is all there is to it. All in all, you will dance for approximately an hour with those twenty-minute dance segments."

"It sounds pretty confusing, Kim."

"Not really. All you need to do is pay attention to yourself and keep an eye on the billboards. Oh, I almost forgot, you will need a name."

"A name? I can't use my name?"

"No, Angela. None of the girls go by their real names. It is a privacy thing. There is no need for the patrons to know your real names. You can imagine why?"

"Yes, I guess I understand. So, what will my name be?"

"I was thinking maybe 'Pink' or 'Raven'. Something like that."

"I think I would like to use 'Raven' for my name. 'Pink' makes me feel like I am boasting about a part of my body. Given this outfit, I surely don't want to entice those patrons any more than they already will be," says Angela.

"Suit yourself, Angela. Will I see you tonight? Remember all dancing starts at 7:00 on the dot. I believe you will be up to dance in the second set. Being new at this, we don't want you to be first up on your first night of performing."

Chapter Thirteen

RICHARD AND THE OTHER PATRON

"Amanda, I am not leaving you out of this sting. Richard will be a patron, and Bobbie will be at the bar trying to get names of the king players. I will be outside the establishment to view anything out of the ordinary. I would like you to mingle among the patrons and enter into conversations to get information that may be important to us."

"OK, Julia, I can do that. Besides, I will be able to keep an eye on my sister as well," says Amanda.

"Richard, it is 6:45. Are you in place?"

"Yes, Julia, I am on the floor center stage."

"Bobbie, have you readied yourself at the bar?"

"I just wandered in, Julia. A few guys are eyeing me. I am sure I will get some information from their conversations. Hopefully, the conversations won't be entirely about me and what they would like to do with me."

"I am sure you can handle it, Bobbie."

"Just don't tell Richard, Julia."

"Amanda, you good?"

"Yes, Julia, I seem to have the same issues as Bobbie. I don't know whether these guys want to watch the dancers or watch me."

"Ladies and gentlemen, thank you for coming out this evening for a good dose of entertainment. As usual, we will have twenty girls dancing for your entertainment. Keep in mind our tipping policies given to you at the door when you entered. If you are ready, I would like to introduce you to the first round of dancers."

"So, what do you think about those girls up there?" asks a patron.

"Every one of them will bring a nice price," says Richard.

"What do you do when you win one of those bitches?"

"One? Hell, I usually take at least four with me by the time those performances finish," says Richard.

"You win the auction for three or four of those beauties?"

"Hell yes, I have buyers that pay top dollar. After all, isn't that why we are in this business?" asks Richard.

"It isn't the only dividend to winning the auction."

"What do you mean?" asks Richard.

"Well, don't you get a piece of ass before you sell them?"

"No, my buyers want 'hands-off' with my girls," says Richard.

"How would they know whether you fucked them or not?"

"Because they know. It can be read on the girls' faces whether I fucked them or not. It is just not worth it to me. I fuck, no sale, then what am I going to do with them?" asks Richard.

"My buyers don't care, so I fuck them."

"To each their own," says Richard.

"Take a look at 'Pink Beauty' at pole 15. She will bring a high price. She has tits and an ass of a twenty-two-year-old, and I bet she isn't over the age of fifteen," says the patron.

Chapter Fourteen

THE BAR CONVERSATION

"Hey, sweetheart, what brings you out on an evening like this?"

"I like watching those girls over there. It is a good excuse to come in here and drink," says Bobbie.

"Well, maybe you could persuade the establishment to allow you to dress, or should I say, undress and grab one of those poles over there. I bet you can wiggle that ass of yours quite nicely."

"I don't think they would want me. I am well over twenty, and those girls look younger than that," says Bobbie.

"Hell, maybe later you can come over to my place and dance with me. I am sure I can find a pole for you to dance with."

"Don't flatter yourself, mister. You are not quite my type. By the way, do you frequent this establishment regularly?"

"Yes, I do, honey. I am here whenever it is open. I win many of those bitches…"

"You what? You say you win some of those girls? How old are those girls anyway?"

"You don't come here often?"

"I come here quite regularly, but don't pay too much attention to the dancers," says Bobbie.

"Well, you see, at the end of the performances, the auction starts. The highest bidder wins the girl or girls they are bidding on?"

"What the hell? You are telling me that those dancers out there are for sale? Do they know it? Do they know they are dancing for an auction?"

"They come here to get work. I, and most of the people here, are employment recruiters, and we use this auction to win girls for our employment pool. We give them jobs. Every one of them is guaranteed work."

"But why a pole dancing performance? Why not just recruit like another outfit?"

"Because those girls come here looking for all sorts of modeling careers, and that is just what they do for them. They give them the start of the career they are looking for."

"How old are those girls? They look like they are twenty, twenty-two, maybe nineteen?" asks Bobbie.

"If you are wondering whether they are legal, well, yes they are. All of the girls are of age, and most are in their twenties."

"But you buy them with money? That in itself is a little shady, wouldn't you say?"

"Listen, you are quite curious about all of this. What is your aim with all of these questions? Are you a cop?"

"Hell no! I don't have anything to do with the cops. I have had many run-ins with them, and I am sick of them sticking their nose in my business," says Bobbie.

"Oh, what kind of trouble?"

"I work the streets…"

"Well, then, if that is the case, you won't mind getting together later? I can pay you."

"Look, I am a hooker, but I like women. Do you get it?"

"Wow-ah! I love seeing lesbians getting it on with each other. Oh, and just to answer your question about the method we pay for the girls, they use a bidding system, and whoever is the highest bidder wins the girl. The monies the high bidders pay goes to the career-building schooling they are promised when they are hired.."

"How does the establishment make money?"

"It is taken at the door, honey. I have to pay the price to come in here and bid."

"I didn't have to pay anything to walk in here," says Bobbie.

"That is because you are not bidding."

"I wonder if I could become a bidder and win some girls. It sure would beat the streets," says Bobbie.

"Holy hell, girl! You are talking about winning some of those girls so you can fuck each other?"

"Why not?"

"For a minute, I thought you were trying to see if all of this, here in this establishment is legit, and you are talking about non-legitimate stuff!"

"Hey, it would be a great way to meet my ladies," says Bobbie.

"Look, I don't want to know your business. All I want is a fuck. Are you sure you couldn't bend your rules, so to speak, and give me a good fuck? I am itching to see what you have under that pair of Hot Pants™."

Chapter Fifteen

ANOTHER CONVERSATION WITH A PATRON

"Excuse me, what are you doing copying down the names of the dancing girls?" asks Amanda.

"Well, these are the girls I will be bidding on."

"What happens to the girls you win? I assume you are referring to an auction?" asks Amanda.

"You must be new here. Almost everyone here knows about the auction and where the girls go."

"Yes, I am new to this establishment. I came here to learn more about the process or auction. I would like to get in on the action. I need some of those girls," says Amanda.

"Oh, really, who do you work for?"

"I don't work for anyone. Why, do you work for someone?" asks Amanda.

"Yes, I have a group who I give the girls I win, for their needs."

"And what needs are those?"

"Listen, my dear, how would you like for me to hook you up with someone in the group? You can make a lot of money, a lot more than going it on your own. Here, take this number and give them a call. I will let them know, and they will be waiting for your call."

"What do you think of number ten and number eighteen? They have great features and are very well toned," states Amanda.

"I agree with you on those two. You have a knack for this business."

Chapter Sixteen

THE HIGH BIDDER

"*A*nd now, ladies and gentlemen, we now are showcasing some of our newer gals for your entertainment."

"Richard, get ready. I think this group of girls will include Angela," says Julia.

"I am ready, Julia. She just came out, and she sure as hell has hardly anything on."

"Hang in there, Richard. It will be all over soon, and Angela will be home safe and sound."

"Ladies and gentlemen, as our evening of performances come to a close, let me remind you the auction will begin soon after. As usual, we will bring the girls out for you to see them for one last time, and then the auction will begin. After each winning bid, we ask the young ladies to remove themselves from the floor and head to their dressing rooms until the entire auction has completed. At that time, your young ladies will be ready for transport."

"Richard, we have a change in plans. I did not anticipate the separation of the girls from their purchasers. I will see if Amanda can get in an area by the dressing rooms and hopefully keep an eye on Angela. I am starting to have a bad feeling about this," says Julia.

"Amanda, are you able to depart towards the dressing rooms?"

"I know where the dressing rooms are Julia. I saw some girls leaving there earlier in the evening. I think the ladies' room is near that area."

"Great Amanda, try to keep an eye on the dressing rooms. Let me know if you see anyone except a female enter."

"OK, Julia."

"Do I hear one hundred twenty-five thousand for 'Stardust'? Going once, going twice, sold to the gentleman with the red coat for one hundred twenty-thousand. 'Stardust', you may exit to the dressing room."

"Julia, I don't understand why these girls are taking the auction seriously. They are not protesting to this human trafficking."

"Richard, we heard from Angela's 'bug', that the girls would get a bonus payment if a patron votes on them. They have no idea that the auction is a sale block. They think the selection process is for the bonus money," says Julia.

"Ladies and gentlemen, let me introduce to you one of our newest girls. Raven put on such an excellent performance tonight. Let the bidding begin. I hear one hundred thousand from the gentleman over there. Do I hear one hundred twenty? I hear one hundred twenty-thousand over there. Do I hear one hundred twenty-five? I hear two hundred thousand from the gentleman with the hat. Do I hear two hundred twenty-thousand? I hear three hundred thousand."

"Richard be careful. You do not want to run out of money."

"I know Julia, but there is this guy a few feet over from me who stares at me every time I make a bid, and he raises me. I think he wants to win her."

"Just keep the raises by only a couple of grand. You cannot run out of money."

"Do I hear three hundred twenty-five thousand?"

"Look, mister, I don't know what the hell you are doing, but I want that bitch!"

"Hey, I am not doing anything wrong. I am just bidding the auction like everyone else in here," says Richard.

"Well, I will warn you, she is mine, and you had better stop raising my bid or else you will hear from my boss, and you don't want to hear from him if you know what I mean."

"Why are you so intent on winning the bid for her?" asks Richard.

"They made her look older than she is, and I would guess not a day over fourteen. She will bring lots of money for my group."

"I have no boss over me. I am going to sell her for sex," says Richard.

"I am warning you! If you are from around here, you must know the law enforcement participates in this auction and doesn't bother this establishment selling these girls for sex. My boss is the Chief of Police and if you think you will rat on me, think again. There is no one to run too."

"I don't give a damn who is bidding. I am just bidding per auction rules, and unless you are ready to put up a huge amount of money, Ravin is mine," says Richard.

"Do I hear three hundred twenty-five?"

"I hear three hundred seventy-five from the gentleman over there. Do I hear four hundred thousand? Going once; going twice.."

"Six hundred thousand," shouts Richard.

"Do I hear six hundred twenty-five? Going once, going twice. Sold to the gentleman with the hat for six hundred thousand!"

"Richard, that was a close one. You only had six hundred thousand at your disposal," says Julia

"I know Julia, but this guy is threatening me to let him win Angela. He said his boss is the Chief of Police."

"So that is why the law enforcement turns a deaf ear to this establishment. We have some big fish to fry with this one."

"Get her out of there as fast as you can, Richard," says Julia.

"Listen, mister, I warned you. Raven is mine!"

"Sorry, but you didn't win her. I did, and I suggest you back off. Get yourself another bitch. There are plenty to pick from," states Richard.

Chapter Seventeen

WE LOST HER

"*I* want to thank you, ladies and gentlemen, for another successful night. Please report to the payment office to present your payment for the girls you won. As soon as the payment clears, you will be escorted to the exit parlor where you can pick up your young ladies."

"Amanda, is everything clear?"

"Yes, Julia, no one has entered the dressing room except the young ladies."

"Were you able to see Angela?"

"Yes, she entered the room just a little while ago."

"Be careful in this very critical time. Richard has to remove her fast and safely. I have a feeling there is someone else after her."

"Oh, Julia, please do not tell me that!" exclaims Amanda.

"Sam, why the hell did you lose that bid for the girl, Raven?"

"I tried, but that guy had a lot more money than we had for her."

"I told you to warn and threaten him!"

"What do we do now?" asks Sam.

"Look, you go to the payment office and delay that guy. I will go to the exit parlor and escort Raven out."

"How the hell are you going to do that? We didn't pay for her," states Sam.

"I am a police officer. If I tell them I will escort her on my behalf, they know better than to question me."

"What is that guy's name?"

"I think he said his name is Richard."

"You are not the gentleman who is supposed to be escorting me," says Angela.

"Look, I just spoke with him, and he asked me to escort you for him. We will meet him out in the car."

"Richard, quick! Someone is taking Angela. I have a hunch; it is the guy that was threatening you!"

"That can't be. I am on my way out the door right now," Julia.

"Richard, I will try to intercept them. I am right outside the front door where all of the sold girls are exiting with their buyers. I don't want to blow our cover, but I just may have too."

"OK, Julia, I will pick up Amanda and head for the exit to meet you."

"Mister, where are you taking me? You are not the person who was to pick me up. You didn't win the bonus vote," says Angela.

"Hell, you believed them? There is no bonus vote, as they lead you all to believe. You have been auctioned off for services," says Chuck, the policeman.

"What services are those?" asks Angela.

"Well, honey, when we get to our destination, I will show you."

"Julia, where is she now?" asks Amanda.

"I don't know. The 'bug' has stopped broadcasting."

"They must have exited out another door. What do we do now, Julia?" asks Richard.

"We need to go back to the office and sort this whole thing out. We have to act fast," says Julia.

"Amanda, please do not worry. We will get your sister back before she is in danger," says Bobbie reassuringly.

"She is in danger now!" exclaims Amanda.

"Hey Sam, get some clothes for her. At least get her a coat," says Chuck.

"What happens to me now?" asks Angela.

"Well, I think you and I are going to get acquainted with some kissing to start."

"You are not the police!" exclaims Angela.

Chapter Eighteen
HUGO WARNS CHUCK

"Sam, call Hugo to find out what he wants us to do next," says Chuck.

"Hugo, this is Sam. Chuck is looking for the next move."

"Let me talk to him, Sam."

"I wish I could, but I think he is busy with that bitch."

"Sam, get him the hell on this phone now!"

"Chuck, Hugo wants to speak with you."

"What the fuck, did you tell him I am busy? Sweetheart, we will continue after I take this call. While you are waiting, take off that outfit."

"Sam, keep an eye on her. Don't you dare touch her. She is all mine. Don't even look at her when she takes those skimpy clothes off," says Chuck.

"Hey, Hugo, what's up?"

"Listen, you moron. The first thing is you are not to touch that bitch! I don't want you inside her! She is not to be spoiled in any way, so put your cock back in your pants and leave your hands off of her."

"Oh come on, Hugo!"

"You heard me, Chuck. Now how is she? Did you get the cream of the crop?"

"She is beautiful, not more than fourteen. It is all I can tell you since I can't undress her," says Chuck.

"Good, she will be going to one of our top whore houses. She will bring them a lot of money, and we will get top dollar selling her to them," says Hugo.

"If she is just going to a whore house, then why can't I fuck her to get her juiced up for them?"

"Chuck, she is going to a place internationally, and they want pure and clean girls only."

"How are they going to know she is pure and clean. It's not like I will leave my fingerprints in her," says Chuck.

"Let me put it to you this way, Chuck, they have ways, and I am not one to argue with them. Now, feed her and get her some respectful clothes to wear. They do not want to receive her in that skimpy dance outfit," says Hugo.

"When is she to be transported?" asks Chuck.

"Just get her ready, and maybe by the end of the week, she will be picked up. I will be in touch. And, by the way, if you lay one hand on her and poke her with your cock, she will tell when I ask her. You will be finished as a partner, and you will owe me her sell price. What was it? Six hundred thousand dollars? You know you don't have that kind of money, so go down the street and find yourself a hooker for a hundred a fuck to satiate your desire for her," says Hugo.

Chapter Nineteen

JULIA GOES ABROAD

"Ok, guys, what do we know so far?" asks Julia.

"We know the law enforcement in that area is involved with the sex trafficking," says Richard.

"The guy at the bar more or less admitted the establishment is part of sex trafficking by supplying underage girls," says Bobbie.

"My observations found that only about ten of the twenty girls are sold at auction. Many of the patrons appeared to be at that establishment just to watch the dancers and not participate in the auction," says Amanda.

"I would guess that the only patrons partaking in the auction are law enforcement in that area," says Julia.

"So, who has her now?" asks Amanda.

"It would be the guy threatening me for winning the bid for Angela," says Richard.

"During conversations at the bar, I got the indication this sex trafficking ring is huge, and many of the girls are sold to the internationals," says Bobbie.

"I need to visit that establishment and find out where those girls go and who is responsible for the transfer," says Julia.

"What is your plan?" asks Richard,

"I'm an International Diplomat, and someone stole my girl," states Julia.

"May I help you, ma'am?"

"Yes, I want to speak to the top man or woman of this establishment," says Julia.

"And who are you, if I may ask?"

"My name is Antoinette, and I am the Ambassador of Sairze, Turkey."

"Wait here. I will bring him."

"Miss…"

"Just call me Antoinette."

"What is it you want from me, Antoinette?"

"I am the Ambassador of Sairze, Turkey, and I believe you sold a girl of ours to a supposed police officer?"

"Well, we did sell a girl to a police officer, but he won her fair and square for six hundred thousand dollars."

"My understanding is this police officer stole her from the person who bid the six hundred thousand dollars and won her."

"We don't pay that close of attention. All we do is register who won which girls and then when payment is complete release the girls to their purchaser."

"My country is not going to be very happy to hear this. I am here to retrieve our girl."

"Well, Miss…"

"Antoinette."

"Well, Antoinette, I wish I could help you. Here, take my card. If there is any way further I can help you, please call me."

"You can help right at this moment. What Internationals do these girls get sold too?"

"How do you know Internationals are the purchasers? A policeman from this area bought her for himself, I assume."

"I know that Internationals purchase ninety percent of your girls," states Antoinette.

"I don't know for sure, but I know many patrons, here, are purchasing the girls for a career opportunity for a few Princes in Saudi Arabia."

"Why is this girl so important to you? We have plenty of other girls here, and I would be willing to give you one to your liking."

"The Imperialist has requested this girl by the name of Raven. He has connections who have given him all of the required bios of this girl. He does not want a substitute."

"I understand Antoinette. Raven is one in a million. She is one or two steps above all of our girls. She would do your Imperialist well and good. She is a faithful one."

"Hey guys, I am on my way to Saudi. I have information that Angela was sold to Internationals, and she is on her way to Saudi. I hope I can arrive there before she arrives," states Julia.

"Julia, do you need help with this?"

"No, Bobbie. I wish you guys could accompany me, but there isn't time. I can't let them get their hands on Angela. If you don't hear from me within a week, it may mean something went wrong. Hopefully, that won't happen. Amanda don't worry. I will get your sister back to you."

"Thank you, Julia. If you need help, I will be the first one there."

"Sit tight, Amanda, I will be all right."

Chapter Twenty

JULIA LANDS IN SAUDI

"*M*iss, please state your business to our country."

"My name is Antoinette, and I am the Ambassador for Sairze."

"Why are you visiting?"

"I am here to visit a friend of mine."

"How long are you staying?"

"Probably for just a few days."

"May I see your Visa, please?"

"Can you tell me, sir, where the top-grade casinos are located?" asks Antoinette. "I want to take my friend to the best casino you have here."

"At that monument over there, follow the road to the right. At about ten miles, you will have arrived at the very best casino we have in this area. Does your friend live in this area?"

"Yes, she does. One more question, please. Are shipments to the Imperialists come by boat or by air? I have furniture being shipped here, and I was told it wouldn't get here soon enough for my visit, so they transported it via the Imperialists. I have no idea what that is."

"I am not sure. Shipments come by boat and by plane. It all

depends upon the cargo. Your furniture probably came by boat. The dock is located about fifty miles from here."

"I thought it is coming by plane."

"I have not witnessed any such cargo on a plane."

"Thank you," says Antoinette.

"Your very welcome, ma'am. I hope you have a lovely stay here."

Chapter Twenty-One

AT THE SHIPPING DOCK

"Sir, where can I find the shipping dock? I shipped some furniture, and I understand the delivery was to be by ship," says Antoinette.

"Ma'am, there have been no shipments arriving with furniture. At around six this morning, a ship docked, but there was no sign of any furniture."

"Are you sure there was no furniture on that shipment? I was assured it would arrive by ship. When does another ship dock today?" asks Antoinette.

"There are no other ships to port today. As I said, the only ship today was at six this morning, and there was no furniture on it. All that came off the ship were a bunch of girls."

"A bunch of girls?"

"Yeah, many ships dock here with young girls."

"Why so many girls? That seems strange," says Antoinette.

"I don't know. Maybe visitors?"

"Have you ever seen bunches of girls board and ship out? Where are these girls coming from?"

"Those girls appear to come from all over. There are many races, colors, ages; you name it."

"Once they land here at this dock, where do they go?"

"I don't know. Shortly after they arrive here, a van comes, and they board and off they go. Why are you so interested in those girls?"

"The furniture I am waiting for belongs to a friend of mine over here in Saudi. I was just curious about the shipment of girls when you mentioned it," responds Antoinette.

"If you don't mind, I have some paperwork to complete. It was nice talking to you."

"Would you mind calling for a taxi?" asks Antoinette.

"Sure, I can do that. Where are you going?"

"I am going to meet my friend in town here."

"Lady, did you call for a taxi?"

"Yes, I did, but I was expecting a taxi, not a van with no company name on it," says Antoinette.

Chapter Twenty-Two

THE TAXI RIDE

"You definitely must not be from around here. In this area, taxis here are independent and not owned by a company. This van is all I can afford, but I assure you I can take you where you want to go."

"I need to get to town. I am meeting my friend."

"OK, get in. I will take you there. By the way, I didn't catch your name?"

"My name is Antoinette and yours?"

"Call me Fred."

"Fred, how far is it to the town? My friend didn't give me much direction. She just told me to meet here in this town."

"Oh, your friend is female?"

"Yes, her name is Angela. She is a student at the university here."

"I was thinking you were meeting your boyfriend," says Fred.

"No boyfriends for this lady."

"Why not? You certainly are attractive enough."

"Fred, where are we going? It does not look like anything that resembles a town. It looks more like a desert."

"I will get you to town. I have to make this one-stop first."

"A stop in the desert?" asks Antoinette.

"Yes, just sit tight I will be back in a minute."

"Get out of the van, bitch!"

"What is this? What do you want, and at gunpoint?" asks Antoinette.

"Just get out and get over there!"

"This is an outrage! What is this place?"

"Just get going! Get in there!"

Chapter Twenty-Three

THE DISCOVERY

"What the hell is this? Who are all you girls, and what are you doing here?" asks Antoinette.

"We don't know. We hired on as pole dancers and was supposed to be performing for pay bonuses. We must have been drugged. First, we were at the dance club, and then we woke up here in this...I don't know what you call it, but I call it a jail. There are guards outside this bolted door. They peer at us through that little window and make remarks to us."

"Do you know of a girl named Angela?" asks Antoinette.

"Yes, we have seen her here, but they removed her a couple of hours ago."

"Where did they take her?" asks Antoinette.

"We don't know. We don't even know why we are here."

"Look, I am a Police Chief back in the States, and my name is Julia, but I am using the name Antoinette as an alias. I am here to find Angela and bring her back to the States along with all of you. They have brought you here to provide sex. The dance club is an underground recruiter for sex trafficking, and I was working to break it up by using Angela. Something went wrong, and we lost track of her."

"Sex trafficking? What will they do with us? Force us to have sex?"

"Yes, I am afraid so. What is your name?" asks Julia.

"I am Karen, and over there is Jessica, Linda, Sophie, and Isabel."

"Are there more of you?" asks Julia.

"Yes, there were, but they took them away just before they took away Angela," says Linda.

"So, to answer your question, I believe they have sold you girls to some High Priests or Princes over here, and they will set you up in whore houses to make money off of you. Many times, they will, 'try you out' as they say, before you start accepting male clients," states Julia.

"'Try us out'?" asks Sophie.

"Yes, young ladies, they will often perform sex with you to be sure you are going to bring in money for them. Have they touched any of you?"

"No, but I bet that is where they took the other girls and your girl Angela," says Isabel.

Chapter Twenty-Four

JULIA'S PLAN

"Hey you, guard! I need to talk to you!" exclaims Julia.

"Look, bitch, we will not talk to you, now get over there and don't you try anything!"

"Would you like to change your mind about talking to me?" asks Julia/Antoinette as she lifts the corner of her dress way above her thigh.

"I will see you ladies later," says Julia.

"Yeah, bitch, I will bed you down just like the rest. You may not be as young as them, but I bet you still have a wet pussy."

"Over my dead body, you bastard!" exclaims Julia.

———

"So, what is your name, Miss?"

"What is your name, and why are you holding me captive?" asks Julia.

"I am Prince Jahib. Your name is?"

"My name is Antoinette. Where is Angela?"

"Oh, you know Angela?" asks Prince Jahib.

"Yes, she is my friend, and I came over to your country to visit her," says Julia.

"Well, well, you came to the right place. You see, Angela your friend, has come to me because I bought her."

"You bought her? What the hell are you?"

"Yes, I bought her at a fair price. Luckily for me I didn't have to buy you. I run a very legitimate business here. The girls we buy are from a dance club who hires girls for sex," says Prince Jahib.

"So, you are running sex trafficking?"

"I wouldn't put it that bluntly, Miss Antoinette. The girls hire out for sex, so they know what they are getting into."

"I highly doubt it. I have talked to those girls, and they have no idea why they are here. Angela and those girls hired out at the dance club to dance and nothing more," says Julia.

"So, why are you here? You aren't here to visit Angela. You are here to take her back?"

"Yes, you stole her!" exclaims Julia.

"I did not! I paid a huge amount of money for her. I don't care where she came from or who bought, stole, or whatever. She was for sale, and I made the sale."

"What are you planning to do with her and the other girls?" asks Julia.

"The same thing as we are going to do with you. I don't deal with women your age, but I have a position for you."

"And what is that?" asks Julia.

"What do you think I want with those girls? I am going to sell sex with them," says Prince Jahib.

"You mean you purchased them so you can turn them over to be whores after you are through with them?"

"Yes, Antoinette, and they will bring in a lot of money. You will be their 'momma'."

"Their 'momma'?"

"Yes, Antoinette, you will run the whore house and schedule the girls as needed. Of course, you will service my older clients."

"I will do no such thing!"

"You do not have any choice!"

"Where is Angela? I want to see her right now!" exclaims Julia.

"Oh, she is indisposed at the moment. I am sure she has not completed 'testing'," says Prince Jahib.

"Testing?"

"Oh, yes, we 'test' every one of these girls. We have to be sure they will satisfy our clients."

"You mean they perform sexual acts?" asks Julia.

"You guessed it, and you will also be 'tested'....by me!"

"The hell you will fuck me!" exclaims Julia.

"Guards, take Antoinette, and get her ready for me. No clothes, completely nude. I need to see what age has done to her."

"Angela! Are you OK?" asks Julia.

"Yes, I am scared, Julia!"

"Angela, you will need to call me Antoinette. They don't know me by my real name. Have they touched you? Have you been 'tested' as they say?"

"No, they stripped me down completely and tied me to that bed over there. Something happened, I think. I suspect the guy couldn't get hard enough to enter me. They said something about replacing him."

"That is a godsend! I am here to get you out of here. Unfortunately, they want to 'test' me as well. The Prince claims he is going to fuck me."

"Antoinette, how are we going to get out of here?" asks Angela.

"I have been in similar situations in the past. We have to act fast. We do not have much time. I am sure they will be here very shortly," says Julia.

"What are you thinking?" asks Angela.

"Look, would it be OK with you if I insisted we both are present for the 'test'?"

"Yeah, I guess so. It sounds kinky."

"It is Kinky, Angela. I am going to reveal I prefer lying with women and request we have a 'three-some'."

"Well, I am not a lesbian!" exclaims Angela.

"Nor I, but I have a plan on how to get us out of here. Because I request to have you present for the encounter, I can catch the guy off guard. I promise you I will not ask you to touch me in any of my private parts. I won't touch you either. All you will need to do is start by massaging my lower legs and feet while I ready him to enter me. Don't worry. He will not enter you or me. I will have killed him by then," says Julia.

"But, you said the Prince wants to fuck you."

"I am pretty sure he wants me all to himself, so he won't want to be there when all three of us are present," says Julia.

"But, I am to be 'tested' as well. How is that going to work?" asks Angela.

"He will want to fuck me first. I have ways to sway him to doing me before he does you," says Julia.

"So, how do we do this?" asks Angela.

"You will start massaging my legs and feet. I will start to run my hands through your hair. It will drive him nuts because he wants to fuck you like he is supposed to do for the Prince. We will start with just our underwear. He is going to have to work to get our panties off. I wore a very revealing pair of panties, much like a G-String bikini. He won't be able to resist because I will be seductively moving my thighs, and he will be so eager to get to my crotch that his sexual desire will overcome his reasoning. He will need to beg to get my panties off, and I won't do it. I will entice him to do it for me. I am going to hedge my bets that he will put his nose right down there to smell me before he starts to pull my panties off. Just as he does that, I will pin his neck with my legs until he faints and finally dies due to suffocation," says Julia.

"What if he won't start to remove your panties, and what if he doesn't sniff your crotch?" asks Angela.

"For him to get me to cooperate, and because he will view me as an experienced woman as far as sex is concerned, he will do anything to fuck me with little resistance from me. As far as sniffing me, well because you are young, you probably don't know this, but smelling pussy is the main appetizer for males as part of their foreplay to become aroused. He will sniff my crotch!"

"Well, I guess I am getting a sex education class today," says Angela.

"OK, once we are free from him, we will need to get out and get out fast. The only place we can to go immediately is the desert. It will be getting cold out there, and we will be in the desert for a while. We will bring these blankets with us," says Julia.

"What are we going to do with the body?" asks Angela.

"We will have to drag him partly out to the desert with us. It will slow them down chasing us because they first will try to find out what happened to their rapist and where he went," says Julia.

"Once they tire of trying to find us...I am assuming they will?"

"Yes, Angela, they will tire and stop to get some rest before resuming the hunt for us in the morning. They know the desert better than we do, and they know if they don't find us soon, we will have perished by the frigid night air, and if we survive through the night, we will burn up in the desert sun of the daytime."

"How are we going to get away from this place and the desert?"

"Early morning while it is still dark, we will come back here and take the jeep I saw over in a corner behind this building," says Julia.

"Won't they hear the jeep engine?"

"That is where our strength will have to come in, Angela. We will have to push it some distance before we can start it. As long as they are not alerted, we should be a good distance from here by the time they realize we are missing."

"I wish we could take the other girls, Julia."

"We will, but we have to get safe first, or the rescue of the girls will never happen."

Chapter Twenty-Five

THE LESBIAN SKIT

"All right, bitch, get in the other room. This little sweetheart and I are going to get acquainted. You will get yours with the Prince!"

"Listen, Louie, is it?"

"Yes, how do you know my name?"

"I have ears, you know!" exclaims Julia.

"Yeah, what do you want?"

"You see, Louie, I am quite fond of Angela here, and I, well, you know, I prefer lying with women, although men are OK too."

"So, you two are lesbians?"

"In a way, but that won't stop you now, will it Louie?"

"So, you want to be involved with that bitch while I am fucking her?"

"Well, yes, that is the plan, but one condition, and that is you will fuck me first," says Julia.

"Oh no, you are the Prince's bitch. There is no way I am going to touch you," states Louie.

"How will he know Louie? I won't tell, and neither will Angela."

"No, it isn't going to happen that way. If you want to play with her, while I fuck her, it is OK with me, but just don't get in my way."

"Come on over here, Angela and start with my legs and feet," says Julia.

"Wait a minute, you two. I want you to strip down first," says Louie.

"Oh, Angela, Louie wants us to strip down to our underwear," says Julia.

"No, I want you two to strip down naked."

"Slow down, Louie. It will happen in time, now get yourself ready while Angela and I start to get it on."

"I still think it best to screw her first."

"Aw, come on, Louie. Take a look at this. Do you see anything inviting between my legs?" asks Julia.

"Yes, Angela, that feels good on my feet. As soon as Louie finishes with me, I am all yours," says Julia.

"All right, bitch, spread those legs. Give me room to sniff your crotch."

"All right, Louie, go ahead and tease me before I remove my panties. Take a couple of deep breaths. It makes me 'hot'."

Louie places his hands on Julia's inner thighs and spreads them so he can put his head between her legs and starts to take some deep breaths sniffing her.

"Ah...you are choking me! Release your legs from around my neck!" screams Louie.

"Quick, Angela, hold him down!"

"Keep sniffing, Louie! It will be the last time you smell pussy!" exclaims Julia.

"Release me, bitch.......I can't breathe.…..."

"Did you think we were going to let you anywhere near us, Louie? Just a few more minutes, Louie! Take your last deep breath!" exclaims Julia.

"That does it, Angela. He won't be bothering us anymore."

"How did you do that, Julia? I mean, how do you get the strength in your thighs to tighten enough to chokehold?"

"Yoga, Aerobics, and Kickboxing. You will have to join me in some classes when we get back. Now go ahead and get dressed and grab those blankets over there."

"Where are we taking him, Julia?"

"Let's pull him out this back door, and we will bury him in a shallow sand-covered grave over there in the dune."

"When can we get out of here, Julia. I want to be rid of this place. I am scared they will catch us," says Angela.

Chapter Twenty-Six

THE ESCAPE

"It is pretty quiet now, and it is getting early morning. Let's get to the jeep quickly. I hope you have enough energy to help me push this thing for a bit," says Julia.

"I have energy. Anything to get out of this nightmare," says Angela.

"Let's push this thing over to that slight rise. Hopefully, we can jump in and ride it down the slope far enough so we can start it and get going," says Julia.

"How are you going to start it? There are no keys in the ignition," asks Angela.

"Right under this dashboard, I find these two wires. I yank them out and touch them to each other, and she starts."

"How did you know that, Julia?"

"I am a cop, remember? We know these things."

"OK, Julia, can we get out of her now?"

"Hop in Angela and hang on."

"Where are we going?"

"We are going to the airport and fast."

"How do you know where it is?" asks Angela.

"While traveling here, I took note of the direction and know we need to go east to get to the shipping docks, and from there, I know how to get to the airport."

"How are we going to fly out of here? I have no identification; no passport, nothing," says Angela.

"I took care of all that. I have everything we need locked in a locker I rented at the airport. I knew pretty much what I had to do to get to you, so I planned."

"Julia, what would have happened to us if you weren't able to persuade that guy the way you did?"

"I don't know, Angela, but I was raped once, and that will never happen to me again, and I sure as hell wouldn't let that happen to you. I hope you know that this was not the plan. Richard was supposed to be able to get to you right after the auction and take you to your home safely."

"I know Julia. You guys tried. It doesn't matter. You found me, and we are going home now."

"Luckily, it isn't quite light out here yet. Do you see that lighted area over there on the horizon? That is the shipyard," says Julia.

"Damn, it is cold out here in the desert. My nipples are so erect they are starting to chafe," says Angela.

"It is better than the desert sun," says Julia.

"Do you think they are on us by now?" asks Angela.

"I am sure they are, but we are well ahead of them, and we will be in the air before they get to the airport," says Julia.

Chapter Twenty-Seven

THE SHIPPING DOCKS

"Are you ladies headed to the airport?"

"Yes, we are as a matter of fact," says Julia.

"Boy, have you ladies been riding in the desert all night? You two look very tired and disheveled."

"We kind of got lost out there yesterday. Silly us going into the desert without a GPS, huh?" asks Julia.

"Yeah, I guess so. By the way, you may want to wait to get to the airport."

"Why is that?" asks Julia.

"Something is going on over there. The Prince and his pawns are there. Maybe some of his cargo ran off."

"Cargo!" exclaims Angela.

"Yeah, the Prince invites American girls over here. He promises scholarships to our most upstanding universities. They are just teenagers, they are."

"Look, there probably will be a delay at the airport, and I need to get her back to school in the States. Would it be possible for us to catch a ride on the next ship to America? When is this ship, here, going out, and where is it going?" asks Julia.

"Well, I can't do that for you two. There are strict orders on people leaving our country with no passports and identification unless you do have them?"

"We don't. Dumb us lost everything we had in the desert," says Julia.

"Yeah, I guess so. It looks like you lost your clothes out there as well."

"It gets pretty hot out there. Sometimes underwear is all one needs," says Julia.

"That ship is going to the States, and it leaves within the hour, but I can't let you board."

"Isn't there something we can do to get on the ship?" asks Julia.

"Well, let me think. There just might be…..."

"Look, the deal is you don't touch her," states Julia.

"Anything I want?"

"Anything you want. Is it a deal?" asks Julia.

"Yes, you can sit in my office, missy. And you, my lady, follow me."

"All right, how do you want it? On top, underneath, or in the backdoor?" asks Julia.

"What do you mean, lady?"

"I thought the deal was to fuck me. Look, I can just bend over this counter if you would like. Here, I will take my panties off, and you can have all of me. How about my tits? Want to see them too?" states Julia.

"Lady, please stop! I, I…I am afraid of females. I am afraid of you."

"What the hell is the deal then? I was sure it was to fuck you," says Julia.

"I, I…want you to jerk me off."

"Look, you can stick your dick in my pussy, but I am not sucking your dick!"

"No, no! I don't want you to use your mouth. Use your hand. There is some jell over there for you to use. Yes, I do need to see you with your top off so I can get hard. Stroke it slowly but deliberately."

"One last part of this deal. Your spew cannot land on any part of my body. I will pull away when I sense your moment of ecstasy," states Julia.

"Here, grab hold of me….stroke it slow and steady…..a little faster now. Do you mind if I turn on this fan? I need your nipples erect…I need to see those big beautiful nipples….stroke me a little faster; a little tighter…..I smell your pussy…I taste its discharge….faster and along my entire shaft….it's moving…I can feel it coming….oh, oh, ah…..the release…….."

"Has the deal been satisfied?" asks Julia.

"Yes, it has. Maybe next time, I will get enough courage to fuck you."

"Don't bet on it buddy, I won't be back here. Besides, I would have never let you touch me! Now, get her and me onto that ship!"

Chapter Twenty-Eight

THE SHIP

"Captain, these you ladies are hitching a ride with you to the states."

"Have they been cleared? Can I see their passports?"

"They have been cleared by me! Here, take this!"

"OK, ladies, go ahead and board. Next time Charlie, it will be one hundred each."

"This is highly unusual, ladies. I bring young ladies over here, but they never make a return trip. You two are the first."

"Where can we freshen up?" asks Julia.

"Go on down the hall there, and two rooms will be on your right."

"We prefer to stay together. Thank you."

"You might find some clothes in one of those rooms. It looks like you barely have anything on under those rags of yours. Anyway, help yourself to any you find."

"I am a little hungry, Julia," says Angela.

"Oh, I will bring you some breakfast ladies," says the captain.

"Julia, what did you have to do to get on this boat. You didn't have to,,,,"

"No, let's just say I assisted him in 'getting off' but not in me. Hell, he is afraid of women. He just wanted me to jerk him off, so I did with my hand."

"That is so gross. I am so sorry I got you into this."

"Angela, we got you into this, and I will do everything in my power to get you home unharmed."

"They all seem to be aware of the young girls being brought over here on this ship. I wonder if they know what is going on?"

"My guess is some do, and some have been fed a story," replies Julia.

"Do you think that captain will leave us alone? He was staring at my ass as I turned around. I wish I had my clothes on instead of these skimpy panties," says Angela.

"After dinner tonight, you can get some sleep. I will guard the door. The captain won't bother us," says Julia.

"When will you sleep, Julia?"

"When I can guarantee you are safe."

Chapter Twenty-Nine

THE HUNT FOR THE GIRLS

"Prince Jahib, those girls are not anywhere to be found."

"Did you ask Louie where they are?" asks the Prince.

"He is also missing along with our jeep."

"Scour the area and find Louie! We must find those women. We can't afford them alerting the authorities of our business dealings," says the Prince.

"We found Louie. He has been strangled and buried in the sand behind the building."

"Get the van and find the jeep tracks. We have to find them!" exclaims the Prince.

"With the desert wind, it will be nearly impossible tracing their tracks."

"Make it happen! I do not want to hear excuses," states the Prince.

"Julia, how much longer before we hit landfall in the States?"

"We have about another day to go. This ship is certainly not the fastest," states Julia.

"Prince Jahib, the jeep tracks appear to be heading east."

"The airport! You take four of the men and get to the airport. No one flies out until we find those women!" exclaims the Prince.

Chapter Thirty

THE CAPTAIN

"Yes, captain, what do you want?" asks Julia.

"How are the accommodations? Are you ladies comfortable?"

"We are fine. How long before we make the port in New York?" asks Julia.

"We could be there by tomorrow afternoon depending upon the wind and the current. Would you like a complimentary drink?" asks the captain.

"No thank you, sir. Now, if you don't mind, we would like to get some rest," says Julia.

"One more thing, miss. I need to talk to you about a matter. It won't take long."

"I am sure it can wait until the morning, now goodnight, captain."

"No, I insist! It won't take long. Please come with me to my quarters."

"No, we will go topsides and talk there," insisted Julia.

"Fine. Meet me topsides in five minutes," says the captain.

———

"Julia, what do you think he wants to talk to you about?" asks Angela.

"I am not sure. I haven't seen anyone else aboard this ship. I am sure there are others here. Angela, please lock this door after I leave. I will knock three rapid taps on the door when I return."

"OK, Julia, please be careful!" exclaims Angela.

"OK, Captain, I'm here. What is it you need to talk to me about that couldn't wait until tomorrow morning?" asks Julia.

"I don't have aboard passengers such as you and your traveling companion who don't have the proper paperwork and identification to leave the country. The guy at the shipping dock paid me one hundred dollars to smuggle the two of you. Well, it ain't enough!"

"What do you expect the two of us to do about that?" asks Julia.

"About the only thing to alleviate this is to have you or her, or even both of you, to 'bed' with me tonight."

"If you are talking about fucking me or her, you aren't going to have the opportunity!" exclaims Julia.

"You see, there are others on this ship, and they don't know you two are aboard. The crew about now are hungry for some pussy. They get plenty of it on the trip from the States with the group of girls traveling to the Prince. So, I could tell the crew you two are on this ship, and you would be fucked so much you wouldn't be able to walk. On the other hand, if you agree to fuck me, well…."

"It isn't going to happen, sir! There is no way she or I will let you screw us!" exclaims Julia.

"Come on. You are used to all sorts of guys, the whores you are."

"We are not whores!" exclaims Julia.

"All the girls going to the Prince are whores. What makes you so special?"

"We were over there visiting friends," says Julia.

"Doesn't matter. It is with all those crew males or me, and they won't be as gentle as I will be," states the captain.

"You aren't going to touch my girl!" exclaims Julia.

"Just be up here at eleven tonight, and I will forget about the girl.

Be sure to wear that skimpy outfit you were wearing when you came aboard," says the captain.

"You touch me, and I will kill you! The guy back at the camp who tried to fuck me I killed before he got his cock out of his pants," states Julia.

"Be up here tonight, or I will alert the crew!"

"Julia are you OK? What did the captain want to talk to you about?" asks Angela.

"Short and simple, he wants us to screw him tonight to make up for the limited amount of pay he got smuggling us on this ship," says Julia.

"The hell with that!" exclaims Angela.

"He threatened me that if I refused to fuck him, then he would unleash his crew on us," says Julia.

"What are we going to do, Julia?"

"There is no way in hell he will touch either one of us. We need to get off this ship now!" exclaims Julia.

"It is impossible! We can't swim to shore. We are stuck on this floating jail!" exclaims Angela.

Chapter Thirty-One

HOT COALS

"I think there is a way, Angela. Coal-fired boilers drive this ship. If I could get down to the boilers and start a fire in one of the coal bins, it would create a diversion that just might cause the abandonment of this vessel. We will be on one of the lifeboats," says Julia.

"They will see we are females and rape us," states Angela.

"No, we won't look like females. We will look just like one of them. We have to get dressed like them," says Julia.

"How are we going to get some men's clothing?" asks Angela.

"Leave that to me. It is eight now, and I have until eleven to cause the diversion," says Julia.

"What if I try to find some clothes, Julia?"

"No, stay put. I will be back within the hour, Angela."

"Angela, it's me, Julia, please open the door."

"Am I sure glad to see you. I was afraid I wouldn't see you again."

"Here, put these pants and shirt on, and you will need to tuck your hair up under this hat. Yeah, that's it, you look like a sailor. I will do the same."

"What is the plan, Julia?"

"As I said, I will get down to the boiler room. I am sure they will put me to work. I am going to take some hot coals from the boiler and bury them in the coal bin. The entire bin will be a huge heat bed, and all will need to abandon ship before the burn completely goes through the bottom of the boat."

"How do you know they will leave you alone enough for you to execute your plan?"

"Boiler room work, as far as shoveling coal in the boiler is hot work. The crewman shoveling the coal must be relieved after a certain amount of time. It is too unbearable for anyone to stay in the area."

"What do you want me to do?" asks Angela.

"In about an hour, make your way topsides and kind of just hang out. You should start seeing activity readying the lifeboats. Make sure you get into one," says Julia.

"How will I know you made it on a lifeboat, Julia?"

"Don't worry, Angela. Just be sure you get in a boat. We will meet up when we hit landfall."

"Hey, you! Get down here and relieve the stoker. He has been here too long. Grab this shovel. You will be relieved in about one-half hour. Be sure to keep the coal hot. The captain wants the engines running at top speed to get to the port in New York by tomorrow morning," says a crew sailor.

"Hey, instead of just loitering on deck, get a broom and start sweeping it down. The captain wants this ship in pristine condition when we dock at the port," says a crew sailor.

"OK," says Angela in the lowest voice possible.

"Times up. You go topsides and get cooled down. Grab a broom and help the other guy up there," says a crew sailor.

"Julia were you successful?" asks Angela.

"Yes, as it turns out, it looks as if we will be in the same lifeboat when all hell breaks loose. Here, rub some of this coal dust on your face. It will help your disguise."

"Yeah, Julia, you don't look like a female with your newly acquired 'makeup'."

"I don't know about that, but you look very much like a handsome sailor," says Julia.

"Yeah, well, don't get any kinky ideas!"

"Oh, never Angela. Let's get pushing these brooms before they suspect something," says Julia.

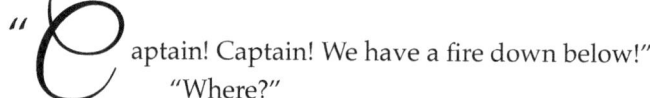

Chapter Thirty-Two
THE FIRE

"Captain! Captain! We have a fire down below!"

"Where?"

"It's in the boiler room...in the coal bin!"

"Can you put it out?"

"No, it has gotten too hot, and the entire bin is on fire!"

"Hell, it will burn right through the hull! All hands on deck! All hands on deck! We have a fire in the hold! Prepare the lifeboats to abandon the ship!" exclaims the Captain.

"You two! Get in a boat. There is no time to lose! The ship is going to sink!" exclaims a sailor.

"Come on, Angela, follow me," says Julia.

"Hey, you! You were down in the boiler room a while ago. How did the coal bin get hot coals into it?" a stoker sailor asks.

"I relieved him, and nothing was burning in the coal bin. I even doused the bin with water as instructed before each shift," says Julia.

"The hell with it! We will never know; she is going to sink," says another sailor.

"Sir, how far are we from the port in New York?" asks one of the sailors.

"We are far enough that we won't make it in this little boat. We will shoot for the Bahamas," says the helmsman.

Chapter Thirty-Three

THE LANDING

"*L*isten up, you sailors! We have landed on one of the islands in the Bahamas. I don't know if the entire crew will show up here, but we will wait to see," says the Captain.

"Angela, get ready to move. We will escape into the dark as soon as we are able. We don't want to be here for the 'role call'."

"Where do we go, Julia?"

"Away from here and to a safe place. There will be lots of questions, and I don't want to face the Captain, even dressed like this. He is a bastard!"

"Julia, that boat just making landfall has, I believe, the captain in it!"

"Yes, you are correct. As soon as the crew moves to the captain for orders, we will slip into the brush. We have to keep together, and we need to get rid of these clothes," says Julia.

"But Julia, I don't have anything on under this clothing except my underwear!"

"That makes two of us, Angela."

"Now, let's go!" exclaims Julia.

"Julia, can we rest? I am out of breath, and we must be quite away from them by now."

"Sure, this is a great place right next to this little pond. Let's get rid of these hats and wash this 'make up' off our faces so we can start looking like beautiful gals that we are."

"Oh, Julia, you are too funny!"

"Well, at least you have a quite colorful bra. It will blend in with some of the attire here."

"Yours isn't that bad, Julia. What are we going to do about the bottom half of us? I am sure the attire here isn't skimpy underwear or 'granny' pants."

"Angela, I have you know, I do not wear 'granny' pants! I just happen to be wearing a thong at the moment."

"Have any of you seen the two girls we had aboard?" asks the captain.

"Two broads aboard captain! We are just hearing about this now?"

"Yeah, I would have fucked them both had I known!" exclaims a sailor.

"Not before I had them in bed! Both at the same time!" exclaims the Captain.

"Wait a minute, Captain, why didn't you tell us about those bitches? How old are they? Are they those fourteen-year-old pieces of virgin flesh?"

"It doesn't matter at this point. Did any of you see the ladies on the ship get into a lifeboat?" asks the Captain.

"Sorry, Captain, they must have gone down with the ship. Such a waste of young pussy!"

"OK, Angela, let's go. Maybe we will find a couple of those colorful wrap-around skirts."

"It looks like we are finally coming into civilization," says Angela.

Chapter Thirty-Four

WELCOME HELP

"*L*adies, your tops are very fitting with our attire, but wearing panties? Those just don't work. You see, in this part of the islands, we like to wear clothes like those who went on before us."

"You wouldn't be like…..be like…..," asks Angela sheepishly.

"No no, my dear. We are very civilized. There are no cannibals here nowadays."

"You wouldn't mind showing us where we can get the proper skirts?" asks Julia.

"Here, you can have these."

"We would like to purchase them," says Julia.

"Nope, they are on the house as long as you two join in the activities tonight. By the way, why are you on this end of the island? Where are you from?"

"We are from New York, and we are actually on our way back there," says Julia.

"So, where is your boat? I assume you came here by boat?"

"Well, we were on a ship headed to New York, but the Captain of the ship, a cargo ship because that is all we could afford, wanted to turn the ship into a floating whore house with us two being the females satisfying all his pleasures and the entire ship's crew's pleasures. We escaped in a lifeboat," says Julia.

"It wouldn't happen to have anything to do with the crew who just landed here a little over an hour ago?"

"Yes, those sailors are the animals!" exclaims Angela.

"Don't worry, ladies. You are safe with us. Let's get you the entire 'costumes'."

"Will they be coming to the festivities tonight?" asks Angela.

"They might, but by the time I get you two dressed and apply some makeup, they won't recognize you."

"The only one who saw us up close is the Captain," says Julia.

Chapter Thirty-Five

BACK AT THE OFFICE

"Richard, I am worried about Julia. Shouldn't we have heard from those two by now?" asks Bobbie.

"Yes, and I am worried about Angela," says Amanda.

"We have no way to contact them. All we can do is wait for their call as planned," says Richard.

"I heard on the news a freighter coming to New York from Saudi sunk due to some kind of fire," says Amanda.

"How are they supposed to get back here? Hopefully, not traveling by way of a boat," says Bobbie.

"Don't start jumping to conclusions, Bobbie. We have no choice but to wait," says Richard.

Chapter Thirty-Six

ISLAND ATTIRE

"**Y**ou ladies look quite smashing!"

"Well, Angela here, definitely looks quite sexy in the grass skirt," says Julia.

"Oh, come on, Julia, you have perfect legs for your grass skirt," says Angela.

"You think so for a thirty-something woman," says Julia.

"Both of you girls look just fine in that attire."

"I would love to have one of these skirts to take home with me," says Angela.

"You both can have those grass skirts and grass tops as souvenirs. I will also give you some clothes to wear, so you don't have to leave here with those crew outfits. Oh, and you can keep the wrap-around skirts as well."

"You are so generous," remarks Julia.

"Think nothing of it. Occasionally that crew makes a stop here, and we all know they are not taking girls over to get enrolled in an educational institute as they lead us to believe. We know they are taking them to their whore houses. What you ladies must have endured; well, you take these clothes with you."

"If it hadn't been for Julia setting the boat on fire, we would have been raped and then sent to one of their whore houses," says Angela.

"Okay, ladies, follow me. It is time to get you something to eat and drink."

———

"Julia, I could get used to living here. Fresh fruit and these vegetables are just so delicious!"

"I agree, Angela, but we have to put a stop to this horror, and we can't with staying here. Besides, I don't think I could get used to running around all day in this skimpy clothing."

———

"Ladies, the festivities are about to start. Don't be afraid of any men here. They have been warned not to try to enter into any short-term relationship with any of us, but they probably will ask to dance with you. You both need to fit in so the crew members won't get any ideas you were the 'cargo'."

Chapter Thirty-Seven

NO SEX TONIGHT

"*H*ey, sweetheart, how about a little chat over there, away from all of this racket?"

"Oh, I see you are one of the crew?" asks Julia.

"Does it matter, missy?"

"No, I guess it doesn't. What do you want to talk about?"

"You see, there were two young ladies on our ship the Captain didn't inform us. In that we had been at sea for a while, well, you know, using the hand gets old."

"So, it sounds like you are asking me if it would be all right to sleep with me?" asks Julia.

"I thought maybe I would ask gentleman-like, but I could force you to spread those legs..."

"What happened to the two ladies on your ship? Wouldn't they take care of your needs?" asks Julia.

"Didn't you see the ship burning out there? Those two bitches burned up, I suppose."

"So, what do I get out of this if I decided to get 'laid'?" asks Julia.

"When is the last time you spread those legs? Don't you think you are about due for some cock?"

"No not really. I can get off as many times as I want. I don't need a cock for that. This cucumber or even this banana works just fine to fill me up," says Julia.

"Yeah, but they can't leave any 'ooze' in you; isn't that what you want?"

"Not me! That is your orgasm, not mine!" states Julia.

"OK, OK, what will it be? Will you fuck me?"

"Hey George, get the fuck away from that bitch! These island girls all have some sort of disease that will eat your cock off if you insert into their glory hole."

"Come on, Frank, you are just jealous because I got to her first!" exclaims George.

"No not really. I got mine from that little sweetheart over there," says Frank.

"She doesn't have the disease?" asks George.

"Oh, I am sure she does, but the disease comes from her pussy, not her mouth," says Frank.

"She gave you a blow job, Frank?"

"Yup, she did, and she swallowed too!" exclaims Frank.

"Well, then, missy, get ready to give me a blow job, and you better swallow too," states George.

"George, I hate to tell you this, but I do women and men. Just a little while ago she and I, well, it was my turn to tongue her pussy...," says Julia.

"You bitch! Come on Frank, let's get the hell away from her. I guess it is back to the hands," says George.

"Angela, you didn't give that guy a blow job?" asks Julia.

"No way, Julia. They think the island girls have some kind of disease coming from their vaginas. I told him I just finished tonguing your vagina. You should have seen him do an 'about-face'. He was just bragging about something that did not happen. Ego trip, you know," says Angela, smirking.

"I told the same thing to them about you," says Julia.

"Maybe we are missing out on something?"

"No, Angela, I don't believe so, I prefer a real man," states Julia.

Chapter Thirty-Eight

THE ESCAPE PLAN

"What is the plan for getting off this island, Julia?"

"She and I...oh, her name is Ariel, talked about it, and in the morning she will have an escort take us to New York. It isn't too far from here."

"But that crew will still be here because of the loss of their ship," says Angela.

"We will set sail before daylight," says Julia.

"Sail? We are going on a sailing vessel?"

"Yes, without a roaring engine, the crew will never hear us," says Julia.

———

"Are you ladies ready? This here is Ronnie. He will be the Captain of the vessel, and I believe you met Wally, he is the one-person crew. I hope your stay with us was at least half-way a good experience considering what you have been through," says Ariel.

"Oh yes, Ariel, we are pleased and grateful for the accommodations and what you have and are doing for us," says Julia.

"Ariel, what is with the supposed disease all of the women on this island carry in their vagina's?" asks Angela.

"Oh, you must have been propositioned from some of the crew last night?" asks Ariel.

"Oh yeah, I was asked to bed down with one of them. He didn't know about the 'disease' because he wanted to get into it with me. One of the other crew came up to us and told the guy about the 'disease'," says Julia.

"Yup, and then they will want to have a blow job," states Ariel.

"We squashed that real quick...we pulled together an excuse that our mouths were contaminated because...," says Angela.

"You told them you licked each other's vaginas?" asks Ariel.

"How did you guess," says Julia and Angela simultaneously.

"It is how our women don't get raped. We started the 'disease' thing, and no one wants to touch them," says Ariel.

"A lot of dissatisfied men coming to this island," says Julia.

"Yup and most of the females on this island are married, and the young girls are taught at a very early age to save themselves for their future husbands. A couple of years ago, some crew stopped by, and one of them tried to rape a sixteen-year-old girl. He did not get back to his ship. We take care of things how we seem fit," says Ariel.

"Let me help you ladies aboard," says Ronnie.

"These two cabins are for you. You will find fresh linens, and we will call you when a meal is served," says Wally.

"We will sail all day and all night. We should be at the port in New York the following day. You are allowed on deck whenever you like, but we ask you to stay in your cabins overnight, and if a storm should come up," states Ronnie.

"Please, ladies, if there is anything you need, do not hesitate to give one of us a call," says Ronnie.

Chapter Thirty-Nine

BOARDED

"Julia, do you feel we can trust these gentlemen on this boat? I mean, as far as not being raped?"

"Angela, I am not sure, but you will bunk with me at night. I think we can trust these guys. Just stay close to me everywhere we go, especially below decks."

"I feel so vulnerable with this wrap-around skirt and panties that fit more like a 'G-String'," says Angela.

"Well, at least you have some material covering down there. I lost mine back there when they tried to rape me."

"You didn't have time to put them back on?"

"No, Angela, the bastard took them as a souvenir. He took them wrapped around his face sniffing as he left."

"Julia, that is so gross! So, you have no underwear at all?"

"I have nothing covering me at all. I am butt naked under this wrap around."

"It must be very drafty?"

"It is not too bad. After all, God didn't intend for us to wear clothes, but if you should see a fig leaf, let me know," laughs Julia.

"Julia, you are so funny at times."

"Angela, I am going topsides to see if they have a radio so I can get a hold of someone in our Department to meet us at the port in New York. As soon as I leave, lock this door. I will knock three times, hesitate, and then knock five times. You will know it is me. Try to get some rest and don't worry. I don't think those guys want to mess with us even though we are almost naked."

"Hey Wally, where is Ronnie?" asks Julia.

"Oh, he is out at the jib trying to tie it down. The wind is coming up, and we want to slow the boat down some," answers Wally.

"Slow it down? Why?" asks Julia.

"There appears a storm brewing, and we can control the boat better with just the mainsail."

"Should we be worried about this storm coming? Are we in any danger?" asks Julia.

"No, just stay in your cabins, and you will be fine. It can be a little rough, and unless you have your 'sea legs,' I suggest you two get topsides when we start to roll and get it over with before you hunker down," says Wally.

"Oh, great! Just what I needed to toss my cookies!" exclaims Julia.

"Happens to the best of us," says Wally.

"Hey Wally, do you have a ship to shore radio? I might as well tell you I am the Chief of Police for the Harford Police Department upstate and need my deputies to pick us up when we land in New York," states Julia.

"What brings you out this way and in Saudi?" asks Wally.

"It is a big issue, and I cannot discuss it with you."

"In there, Miss."

"You can call me Julia."

"The call jingle for us is 'Samantha'," says Wally.

Chapter Forty

THE CALL

"ew York? This is 'Samantha', come in."

"Yes, Samantha, this is New York. How is the sea out there? You need to know a storm is heading in your direction."

"Can you patch me to the Harford Police Department. I am Police Chief Julia Lillus."

"Hang on a minute, ma'am, while I patch you through."

"Hey, Julia! Where the hell are you two?" asks Bobbie.

"We are on our way to New York at this moment."

"We were worried sick. Do you have Angela with you? What happened?"

"Bobbie, I can't go into it right now, but Angela is with me, and she is still a virgin, and I am still an 'after marriage' virgin. We did have some very close calls and could have been very quickly raped. The atmosphere over there...well, we need to get those young girls back and stop the raping because that is what they are doing with them before they send them to whore houses. Bobbie, get the FBI on the line when I hang up and tell them I have all the information they need to shut down this human trafficking ring."

"OK, where do you want to have us pick you up?" asks Bobbie.

"First off, just you and Amanda need come to pick us up. Don't bring Richard! All I can say is both of us are very scantily dressed, and my ass is bare. My panties ended up as a souvenir for a bastard who tried to fuck me. I am too tired to be on the watch that my legs are together in transport, and Richard does not need to be seeing my crotch."

"You got that right, Julia! I will make sure he is not with us, and I will send him home to watch our brood."

"We will be at port in New York City in a couple of days. I will call you when we land. Go on down to the docks in a couple of days, so we won't have to wait very long for you to pick us up," says Julia.

"Julia, are you guys all right? What kind of boat are you on and are you safe with the crew? I am assuming male crew?"

"We are fine and keeping our guard up. There are two of them, and they seem very harmless. We are on a fifty-foot sailboat by the name of 'Samantha'. A storm is heading to us, and the boat is starting to roll. My stomach isn't handling it too well. I will call you Bobbie. Be sure to let Amanda know her little sister was very instrumental in pulling this off, and she is beautiful."

"OK Julia. By the way, watch out when you sit down on the boat. You could sit on a crab, and then you know, you will have a case of the crabs," says Bobbie jokingly.

"Very funny, smart ass!"

Chapter Forty-One

TOSSING COOKIES

"Hey Angela, it is Julia. You need to come with me topsides. A storm is approaching, and I am not feeling too well with all of this rocking."

"I am glad you are here. I was wondering where I can vomit."

"We will go up and heave over the rail," says Julia.

Chapter Forty-Two

RICHARD IS NOT INCLUDED

"Richard, Julia, just called."

"Where are they, Bobbie? Are they all right? How and where are they...how are they getting here?"

"They are fine, and they are arriving in New York by a private sailboat."

"When will they hit land."

"Richard, calm down! They are fine. Amanda and I are going to pick them up in a couple of days."

"What do we do with the kiddos?"

"You are staying at home with them. Amanda and I are going to go."

"But, I want to greet them too."

"Richard put the pieces together in this puzzle, and you will know why you aren't invited. They just escaped a camp where rape is an hourly affair; they don't have proper clothes to wear, and at least one of them has a bare ass."

"You mean....?"

"That is correct, Richard, and you aren't invited. If you desire to see a bare ass, it better be mine and not Julia's."

Chapter Forty-Three

BOBBIE IS HORNY

"Speaking of bare asses, I couldn't help to notice while you were sitting down over there conversing with your sister on the phone, well, you weren't very lady-like and I believe I saw some pink between those legs of yours?"

"You are correct, Richard. I am not wearing any panties, and I was hoping you would notice. I am ovulating and horny as hell. I need to be fucked and fucked hard!"

"Bobbie, are we in need of more children?"

"I am sorry, Richard, but this time you are going to have to wear a rubber or work your magic timing and 'cum' in my mouth. It doesn't matter to me. I am open to anything. I just need to be screwed."

"Beg no more! Hop up here in my arms, and I will take you to my bed, and I will have uninhibited sex with you all night."

"No, Richard! Get on the couch. Right now!"

"OK, my diva, spread those sexy legs of yours real wide and let me fill you up!"

Chapter Forty-Four

THE STORM

"Ladies, I must ask you to get below in your quarters. The storm is approaching very fast. Do you have your sea legs yet?" asks Ronnie.

"I am not sure about that, but we sure have tossed a lot overboard," says Julia.

"Julia, it is your name?"

"Yes, it is, Ronnie."

"Here, take these, and the two of you get down below."

"Julia, make sure to lock the cabin door," states Angela.

"No problem honey; don't be afraid."

"What did that guy give you, Julia?"

"It is a couple pair of shorts, and the kind one puts on before putting on a wet suit."

"Why do you think they thought we needed them?"

"Well, Angela, I am sure when we were hanging our heads over the rail tossing our cookies, those guys got a pretty good look at our asses and mine being bare, well, let's say they got a bonus seeing my .... well you know."

"I never thought about that," says Angela.

"If they don't try to pay us a visit tonight after seeing our asses, I don't think we need to worry about them taking advantage of us," says Julia.

"I don't know how much sleep we will get with this boat rocking like a baby cradle," says Angela.

Chapter Forty-Five

MORNING

"Julia, wake up. Someone is knocking at the door."

"Ladies, are you OK in there? It certainly was a rough storm out there last night. It is a glorious morning with calm waters. We should hit the port in New York before dark," says Wally.

"Thank you. We will freshen up and come topsides in a little while," responds Julia.

"You are welcome to go for a swim if you would like. We have some wet suits here, but of course, they won't help if you want to wash up."

"That is OK. We will be up for breakfast soon," says Julia.

"We could go skinny dipping, Julia," says Angela jokingly.

"Yeah, why not? They have already seen my ass, seeing my breasts are all that is left. I suppose that would be OK."

"Sure, Julia, that suits you, but they haven't seen anything more than my butt cheeks, and I am not willing to show them any more than that," says Angela.

"OK, you smelly girl, let's get up there for breakfast. No shows for them today," says Julia.

"I hope you ladies had a reasonable night of sleep. We have some hull cleaning to do, so we will be out in the water most of the day scraping barnacles. If you would like, we have a cabana up on the foredeck with fresh water. You can freshen up. We won't bother you. If you would like to take in some sun, feel free. When we are ready to board, we will let you know," says Ronnie.

"Thank you. I think we will take you up with that. Angela, if you would like to take a shower I will take the watch to ensure your privacy," says Julia.

"OK, Julia and I will do the same for you."

"Wally, before you go, do you happen to have any sunscreen?" asks Julia.

"Yes, we do. It is in a pouch inside the cabana, along with soap and shampoo. You have the boat to yourself today, so please enjoy it."

"I don't know about you, Julia, but that shower was sure great. I don't stink now. Maybe we can wash our clothes too."

"Look here, Angela. The guys left these here for us. We can get out of these skirts and you out of those G-string panties. The shorts are quite fashionable, and once we put the T-shirts on under these shirts, at least our tops won't show through although they might bounce a bit," says Julia.

"So, what do you want to do today, Julia?"

"Let's explore the boat. I just might want to buy one of these."

"Julia, I know you are the Chief, but I don't think you can afford it."

"I could if I hooked up with a guy such as one of these guys."

"Julia, do you think these types of guys would make a good companion...a lover... a husband?"

"Nope, just kidding. The love of my life is no longer with me physically, but he is still in my heart. That is all I need."

"I am assuming you are speaking of your late husband?"

"Yes, I am thinking of my husband, Tim. I miss him so."

"So, are you going for a tan today?"

"No, I am not going to spend time in the cabin, but I am certainly not going to lay out in the sun either," says Julia.

"Well, you ladies look much more presentable in those," says Ronnie.

"Thank you for lending us these clothes. It was very nice of you," says Julia.

"Oh, you may keep them."

"Thank you," says Angela.

"When do we hit landfall?" asks Julia.

"We should start tomorrow evening. We lost some time cleaning the hull, but it is way too expensive to have the yard do it," says Wally.

"I assure you tonight's sleep will be much better than last night. The seas are very calm now and will be throughout the night," says Ronnie.

"Ron, it looks like we are going to have some visitors. That boat is coming to us pretty fast!" exclaims Wally.

"Oh, no, Julia! They are coming for us!"

"Calm down, Angela. Is there somewhere we can hide? If they are looking for us, they must not know we are on this boat," states Julia.

"Why do they want you two? What kind of trouble are you in?" asks Ronnie.

"Look, we came from Saudi on a mission to stop sex trafficking involving young girls. They grabbed us and pretty much would have raped us and send us to their whore houses if it wasn't for some quick thinking on our parts. We were able to sink their ship, and I am sure they are trying to find us," says Julia.

"No offense, and surely you two are beautiful, but you are not the young type girls you are speaking of," says Wally.

"That group over there are barbarians, and they don't seem to care about the age, and as long as you have boobs and a vagina, then you are to be raped," says Julia.

"Well, we will need to dump your clothes you changed out of overboard," says Wally.

"Do you mind if we do that? You know, it is kind of personal," says Angela.

"By all means, but dump them now, so they are not in sight when the boat arrives in case they are the ones looking for you," says Wally.

"OK, we are going to have to hide you, but it can't be on the boat," says Ronnie.

"What do you have in mind?" asks Julia.

"You take these wet suits and this tank and jump overboard. You will need to hide under the hull of this boat," says Wally.

"Julia, I don't know if I can do that. I am petrified of the water and especially being under it," says Angela.

"Sweetheart, you are going to have to force yourself. The alternative would be just what you escaped from," says Ronnie.

"Angela, you will be OK. I will be right next to you, and you can hold onto me. If you hide onboard and they find you nothing will stop them this time," states Julia.

"Hurry, ladies! Get into those suits, over there on the other side of the boat, and out of sight of the boat coming to us. Once in the water, move under the hull. You will have to share an air tank because that is all we have left. As soon as they are gone, and all clear, one of us will come and get you. Try to be very still and stay right under the hull in the middle of the boat. Now get those clothes and throw them overboard. We have about ten minutes before they will be here. Jump into the water on this side of the boat out of sight," says Wally.

"Do we have to undress to put these suits on?" asks Angela.

"No, no, sweetheart, just put them on over what you are wearing," answers Ronnie.

"Julia, I am so scared. What if there are fish down there…under the boat…sharks?"

"Angela, just stick close to me. You will be OK. Hopefully, it isn't those guys looking for us, and if they are, then hopefully, they won't stay long. Now here goes…jump!" exclaims Julia.

"Ahoy, captain! Permission to board?"

"You may come aboard. Who are you, and what do you want?" asks Ronnie.

"We are with the Saudi Agency of Investigation."

"You are quite far from your country. What do you want with us?" asks Wally.

"Whaaaaat?"

"Shut up and stop asking so many questions!"

"Why have the guns?" asks Ronnie.

"Look, we are going to search your boat!"

"I won't allow it," says Ronnie.

"I don't think you have a choice with this here gun stuck in your back!"

"What are you looking for? Maybe we can speed up the process," says Wally.

"We are looking for two American bitches who we feel are a threat to our security if they make landfall in the United States. One of them is quite tall with jet black hair and a nice-looking ass, and the other is about twenty years old, beautiful and, well, if you were to see her with her legs spread, you would be in some kind of heaven."

"We haven't seen anybody like that, and why do you suspect they are with us on this boat?" asks Ronnie.

"Enough talk now step aside. Men, you two search the front of the boat, and you two search the back. I will search in the middle. Look in all places where a person could hide and look for things that bitches would have, such as perfume, scanty clothing they were wearing when we last saw them, jewelry, things like that."

"I can assure you those two are not on board with us!" exclaims Wally.

"Yeah, that is what you say, but I will bet you have them here, and you have been fucking them! I won't blame you if you have been."

"What will you do with them if and when you find them?" asks Wally.

"Take a guess! Now, where are you hiding them?"

"I tell you we have no idea who you are talking about, and we are the only ones on this boat," exclaims Ronnie.

"Men, do you see any signs?"

"Nothing upfront. We can't even smell any bitches!"

"Nothing back here either!"

"Are you satisfied? You can leave my boat now!" exclaims Ronnie.

"Too bad they aren't here. We could have had quite the party, and all us could have got our fill fucking them before we took them away."

———

"Wally, wait until they are out of sight, and then we will wait another ten minutes before we get those two back on board. We have to be sure they don't circle back," says Ronnie.

"I feel sorry for those two. I'll bet they are the guys who tried to rape them. They are real bastards!" exclaims Wally.

"OK Wally, go fish them out of the water."

"Are you girls, OK?" asks Ronnie.

"Yeah, but I am sure glad to be out of the water," says Angela.

"I'll bet those guys were after us?" asks Julia.

"Yes, I believe so. The description of you fit the bill, but the description of you Angela, well, I would rather not say," says Ronnie.

"I can only guess. By the time I escaped, I didn't have any clothes on," says Angela.

"You ladies were in real danger over there. I am glad you were not hiding on this boat. They would have finished, right here, what they didn't accomplish before you escaped," says Wally.

"Those guys are just part of the sex trafficking ring, and we will put them all out of business as soon as we get back," says Julia.

"OK, ladies, why don't you freshen up, and we will have dinner in about an hour," says Ronnie.

———

"Julia, they seem to be very nice men. I don't think we need to worry about them. I wonder what the description of me was?"

"Well, Angela, being nude, I can only guess....," says Julia.

"I will sleep better tonight knowing that the chances of being attacked are low," says Angela.

"Don't let your guard down yet, Angela. We have just tonight, and then we will be home," says Julia.

Chapter Forty-Seven

POOR YOUNG GIRLS

"Bobbie, I am worried. They were supposed to be at the port yesterday," says Amanda.

"Yeah, I wonder what the delay is," states Bobbie.

"My little sister has been through so much. I worry about her. She isn't very worldly, you know," says Amanda.

"I suspected that when I met her. She has done such nice work for us, and I am sure Julia will agree with us that if it weren't for Angela, we wouldn't be able to break the sex trafficking ring," says Bobbie.

"What will happen to the girls that are already over there when the ring is broken?" asks Amanda.

"Well, they will be rescued and brought back to the states. I am sure every one of them will need to get counseling due to what they made them do over there and find help for those who may be carrying babies with them," says Bobbie.

"It is such a tragedy! Those poor young girls, just children, to have to be violated and then figure what hope is for them in the future," says Amanda.

"Yes, and unfortunately, some of them will continue with what they were forced to learn over there; young little whores," says Bobbie.

"Ladies, we have made you a special 'going away' breakfast. I hope you don't mind a little seafood. It is fresh this morning. I got Wally to do some fishing," says Ronnie.

"We want to thank you for your hospitality. I am looking forward to getting back to my work, but I must admit this type of living on your boat is quite relaxing except for those bastards that invaded our space," says Julia.

"Any time you would like a little vacation, you might want to join us on some island hopping," says Wally.

"You too, Angela," says Ronnie.

"Thank you. I must admit I wasn't very trusting when we started on your boat, but I am OK now," says Angela.

"After what you ladies went through, we can understand the possible mistrust in us," says Wally.

"We will make port in about two hours. The current has been very friendly to us," says Ronnie.

Chapter Forty-Eight

THE PANTIES

"Are you sure you searched every place on that boat for those bitches?"

"I know they were there! I could smell their crotches!"

"We searched everywhere, including all bilge areas."

"Did you see any evidence that those guys were fucking them?"

"No! What did you want us to do? Sniff the sheets?"

"You mean you didn't do that?"

"They were heading for New York. They know too much. We need to get back and let them know we need to lay low. We might even need to move our operations; stop the shipments for a while."

"The Prince won't like that!"

"He is going to have to unless he wants them to come down on him big time!"

"What the hell you got in your pocket?"

"Oh, it is nothing."

"Are you holding out on me? Give it here! What the hell? Whose panties are these?"

"They belong to that young bitch. I believe she was starting to enjoy the thought of me fucking her. These were quite wet with her juices, and boy, the smell of them gives me an instant hard-on!"

"You are sick!"

"You would have done the same thing with that older one if you had the chance."

"Pass them over to me! I want to smell them!"

Chapter Forty-Nine

NEW YORK

"There she is, ladies, the Statue of Liberty. Welcome home," says Ronnie.

"What will you guys do now?" asks Julia.

"We will just head back to the islands and sail around a bit," says Wally.

"Don't forget. We are available if you two want a little boating vacation. Remember ship-to-shore 'Samantha'," says Ronnie.

"OK, thanks again," says Julia.

"Bye now," says Angela.

"Those two are such hot chicks, don't you think, Ronnie?"

"Yeah, I would like to get to know Julia a little more," says Ronnie.

"Do you think they will ever call us, Ronnie."

"I don't know, Wally. We can always hope!"

"Your Passports ladies?"

"Hello, my name is Julia Lillus, and I am the Chief...."

"Yes, we have been waiting for you. Please follow Agent Jones."

"Julia! Angela! We are so happy to see you in one piece! We were worried when you didn't show up yesterday," says Bobbie.

"Angela honey, are you all right? Did they hurt you?" asks Amanda.

"Not physically, but I got first-hand what men are like! They stripped me nude! They saw all of me!"

"Angela, those men are not indicative of all men. Those guys are evil and very twisted," says Amanda.

"After this ordeal, sex is not a top priority to know about," states Angela.

"Honey, when you meet the right man, and you will know he is the one for you, you will have no problems entering into a sexual relationship with him," says Amanda.

"Julia, I see you have some pants? It wouldn't have been to cool meeting Agent Jones with a bare ass!" exclaims Bobbie with a smirk on her face.

"Bobbie, I had a wrap-around skirt covering my ass. It wasn't like I was walking around bare assed. You know there were two guys on that boat," says Julia.

"And......and....what happened, Julia?"

"Absolutely nothing! Those two guys were gentlemen at all times," says Julia.

Chapter Fifty

THE FBI

"*L*adies, my name is Agent Jones from the FBI. Please follow me. We have some questions for you."

"Hello, Miss Lillus and Miss Alexandria. My name is Logan. I want to be the first to thank you so much for getting the information for us to shut down that ring over there in Saudi."

"I have compiled all of the names that will be useful for you to investigate, starting with the Prince down to the men who tried to rape us," says Julia.

"Yes, we are sorry that you two had to be subjected to that. Our plans were never for you to step foot on Saudi soil," says Logan.

"As you probably know, your work in this case is done. We will take it from here," says Agent Jones.

"What will happen to the girls over there?" asks Angela.

"We will rescue them and close down the whore houses. We are prepared to offer assistance to them as far as counseling, baby care, or any other issues that they may have been subjected to," says Logan.

"As far as the part of the ring involved with the shipment of those young women, we have, as we speak, shut down that shipping involvement and have taken all involved into federal custody," says Agent Jones.

"Again, thank you, ladies! You will find something for your troubles on your desk, Miss Lillus," says Logan.

"Ladies, have a good day," says Agent Jones.

Chapter Fifty-One
BOBBIE EXPLAINS

"Bobbie, how did things go in my absence? Anything I need to know about?" asks Julia.

"Well, I am ovulating, and I seduced Richard the other day," says Bobbie.

"Bobbie! How many godchildren do you think I need? Besides, you seduced Richard? Isn't it usually the other way around?" asks Julia.

"Well, yeah, but what is a girl to do? When you need it, you need it!"

"OK, Bobbie. What about police work?" asks Julia.

"Bobbie, I hope I will find a relationship like you have with Richard!" exclaims Amanda.

"Hey, sis, can we talk about something else? I can't stomach anything to do with sex at the moment," says Angela.

"The office has been tranquil, Julia," says Bobbie.

"Bobbie, please drop me off at my house. You, Amanda, and Angela, take the day off and go home. Make it a three-day weekend. I will handle anything that comes in and call you if I need you," says Julia.

Chapter Fifty-Two

SOMEONE IS IN MY HOUSE

"*B*obbie, I am so sorry to call you at this late hour, but I think there has been someone in my house since you dropped me off. I don't think they are still here, and I don't know what they are looking for. It appears they were trying to find some records or maybe addresses," says Julia in a whisper

"Julia, do you want me to come over?"

"No, I believe they are gone. I am going to call Amanda. Do you know if Angela is spending the night with her?"

"I think she said she was," says Bobbie.

"I don't have a good feeling about this. What if they were looking for an address to find Angela?" asks Julia.

"Why would you think that, Julia?"

"I don't think we have seen the last of this sex trafficking case," says Julia.

"How so, Julia?"

"Bobbie, I do not know, but I am leery."

"Amanda, this is Julia. I am so sorry to wake you at two in the morning. Do you have Angela with you?"

"Yes, she, or should I say I wanted her to be with me for a while. She was quite shaken up by almost being raped. She is not very worldly, and she is still a virgin and takes that very seriously," says Amanda.

"Good for her, she is a good girl. I called you to be sure Angela wasn't alone."

"Why is that Julia?"

"I believe someone was in my house since I got home and while I was sleeping. It looks like they were looking for addresses or something. I am concerned someone is looking for Angela and me."

"Do you think this has anything to do with what you were exposed to over there in Saudi, Julia?"

"It might. Please don't tell Angela right now. I don't want to have this add to her stress at this moment. I ask of you to keep her with you for a while and bring her with you when you come to the office. I was thinking of asking her something anyway."

"Ok, Julia, I can do that. Take care and keep me in mind if you need anything."

"I will, Amanda. Good night...or I mean good morning!"

Chapter Fifty-Three

THE CONFRONTATION

"Who is there? I asked who is there?" asks Julia.

"My...my name is Charlie."

"What are you doing in my house; in my bedroom?"

"I was sent to get something."

"Who sent you, and what do you need to get from me?"

"I don't know who it was that gave me the directions. He called me on my phone."

"What did this unknown person want you to do?"

"He wanted me to find you and the other girl."

"What other girl?"

"I don't know. He didn't tell me. He said that once I found you, I would find the girl."

"I don't know who you are and what you want, but you need to get the hell out of my house! I am the Chief of Police. I don't think you realize who you are messing with."

"They will be here! They will be here any moment!"

"Who will be here?"

"They will. I have to do this, or they will kill me."

"Buddy, you are not making sense!"

"They told me they would pay me very well as long as I did this."

"As long as you did what?"

"They told me I needed to get one of your....well, you know....your underwear...."

"Are you referring to my panties?"

"Yeah, and I needed to bring them to him."

"Why didn't you just steal a pair while I was sleeping instead of all of this ruckus?"

"Because......because......because they had to have something on them and then they would know I did it."

"Did what?"

"They told me I had to...well you know...ahh...ahh, I don't want to, but they will kill me. There has to be....ahh...ahh...that stuff on your panties that shows proof..."

"Are you here to rape me, Charlie?"

"I don't know. They told me I had to do it to you and to make sure it got on your panties."

"Listen here, Charlie, you are not going to do it to me..."

"I have too; they will kill me."

"Wait a minute. It appears they found you to find me, and if you raped me, it would be proof that I am here?" asks Julia.

"They said that if I just told them your address, it wasn't enough proof. I...I....don't want to do it. I...I...don't know anything about you girls.....I don't know what to do."

"Shh! I hear something. Don't say anything, Charlie. Stay here in my bedroom. I am going to see what is making the noise."

"They are here. I told you..."

"Shh, Charlie! Stay here while I check the door."

"Hello there, bitch! I bet you thought you would never see us again."

"You had better let me go! I will scream," shouts Julia.

"Oh no, you won't. This here knife is very sharp, and I am not afraid to use it. I could slit your throat, and your pussy will still be wet and warm."

"You aren't going to touch me!"

"No, I am not, at least for now. You see, I hired Charlie, here, to pump his load into you first and then Fred, John, Joe, and I will take our turns. You see, Charlie is going to get you wet for us. We are going to finish what we started over there in Saudi."

"You won't get away with this," says Julia.

"Where is that other bitch? I am sure she has a tighter pussy than yours seeing you were married before."

"You will never get to her. You will have to kill me first."

"We just might do that. I hear she is staying with a big sister. It is said that the big sister is a looker. We just might have to fuck her too."

"The last person who tried to rape me didn't fare very well; actually, I believe he is dead," states Julia.

"Shut up! Charlie, where the hell did you go? Get out there and get yourself ready."

"I....I...don't want to do this. She...she...is a good girl...I...don't want to do it."

"It is easy, Charlie. First, you rip that nightgown off of her, and then you pull her panties off if she is wearing any. Then you will push her down on the bed and spread her legs. You stare at that glory hole of hers, and I am sure you will find that little pecker of yours will rise to the occasion."

"No...no...no...I won't do it. I can't. I have never done that to a girl."

"Charlie, you will do it! Now rip off her robe! Here, I will help you."

"RICHARD! RICHARD! WAKE UP!" exclaims Bobbie.

"What do you want, sweetheart? Don't tell me you are horny at three in the morning."

"Richard, I am not joking. I am worried that something is about to happen to Julia. I can't explain it now, but I need to get over to her house and check on her."

"Should I go with you, Bobbie?"

"I think you should. I will wake my sister and let her know to watch our kiddies."

"Good thing she is visiting at this time," says Richard.

"Now push her down on the bed, Charlie, and pull those panties off of her. It helps if you smell them."

"Richard, I don't like the looks of this. There is a light on in her house, but something doesn't look right. I will go to the back door, and you wait at the front door. You will be my back-up."

Chapter Fifty-Four

THE ASSAULT

"See Charlie, that wasn't so, bad was it?"

"Joe, make sure the gag is tight on her. I don't want to hear anything from her. Fred, thanks for keeping her down with the help of John. She sure is a kicker."

"Can I suck her tits while Charlie is fucking her?" asks John.

"No! You need to help Fred keep her down."

"Charlie, take a good whiff of her panties and spread her legs. Take a look at that, gentlemen! We have finally seen her cherry!"

"Richard, I am going in, as soon as you hear I am inside, break in the front door. Guns raised!" exclaims Bobbie.

"OK, Charlie, now just take your stiff pecker in your hands and guide right there between her legs. Push it in as far as it will go."

"No...No...I can't."

"Yes, you can! Now stick your cock in her!"

"HOLD IT! DON'T THINK OF IT! Richard, stay out there! DROP THE KNIFE!" exclaims Bobbie.

"Are you OK, Julia? Hey, you with your pants down and your cock sticking out, take the gag out of her mouth."

"Richard close your eyes...," says Bobbie.

"I am OK, Bobbie. Richard get in here and cuff these bastards!" exclaims Julia.

"JULIA! OH SHIT, JULIA!"

"What is the matter, Richard? Haven't you seen a bare ass of a female before?" asks Julia.

"Here, Julia, take your robe," says Richard as he passes Julia's robe to her.

"What do you want me to do with this guy...PULL YOUR PANTS UP! WE DON'T WANT TO SEE YOUR PECKER!" exclaims Bobbie.

"You don't need to cuff him," says Julia.

"But he was about to stuff himself into you!" exclaims Bobbie.

"He wasn't going to do it. They were pushing him to do it. He wouldn't have done it."

"Charlie, please have a seat on the bed and relax. You aren't in any trouble, but we will need to ask you some questions later," says Julia.

"Julia, do you know who these guys are?" asks Bobbie.

"Yes, they are the ones over in Saudi who attempted to rape Angela and me."

"I thought that was all over...," says Bobbie.

"It will never be over. All you bitches need to be fucked, especially you, redhead with the tight ass."

"SHUT UP, YOU BASTARD!" screams Richard.

"Take it easy, Richard! Listen, buddy. You seem to have a sex problem. Do you want to rape? Just wait because where you are going, you will have plenty of opportunities to have your fetish satisfied!" exclaims Bobbie.

"OK, Bobbie and Richard, take them to the cell. I will turn them over to the FBI in the morning. I am going to take a shower. Thank you, guys!"

"I had a hunch you weren't safe here. What do you want us to do with Charlie?" asks Bobbie.

"Nothing. Leave him here. I want to talk to him. I will take him home when I am done. I am not going to charge him with anything," says Julia.

"Charlie, in case you didn't catch it, my name is Julia, and I am the Police Chief here in Harford."

"Miss Julia, I wasn't going to do it....I....I....couldn't. I didn't breathe in your pants when they told me too. I held my breath. I didn't want to see it...I didn't want to see..."

"Didn't want to see what Charlie?"

"That....that....that...thing between there."

"That's OK, Charlie, you weren't going to do anything with that thing. You are OK."

"No...No...No...I wasn't going to do what they wanted me to do. Why did they want me to do that to you? How come they wanted me to put my....my....thing in that?"

"Don't worry about it, Charlie. They are bad men, and they won't be bothering you anymore. Are you OK now, Charlie?"

"Yes...Yes...You are my friend. Can I be friends with you, Miss Julia?"

"Yes, you can, now how did you meet these guys that wanted you to do those things to me?"

"They just came up to me on the street and promised me a lot of money if I would do something for them. They never told.....told....told....me what they wanted me to do."

"Charlie, I am going to take a shower, and then I will take you home. Please have a seat on the couch out there, and I will be out in a few minutes."

"Oh Timothy....you are the love of my life....oh Timothy," Julia sings as she soaks herself in the shower.

WHAT THE HELL?

"Who is out there?" asks Julia as she sees a silhouette of a person outside the shower curtain.

"Charlie, is that you? What do you want? Please go out to the living room, and I will be done in a few minutes."

"CHARLIE! WHAT ARE YOU DOING? CLOSE THAT CURTAIN AND GO TO THE LIVING ROOM!"

"Pretty good, huh, bitch? And you believed every bit of the shit I told you. My name is Randy. Charlie is this little retarded kid who couldn't get his cock stiff if he tried."

"GET OUT OF HERE!"

"Who is going to help you now, bitch? I have you all to myself, and I get the prize now that you are completely nude. Lower your arms and let me gaze at your tits."

"No, I won't!"

"Come on, do I need to get you to do what I want with this knife? Why don't you be nice and cooperate? I just want to take a shower with you."

"Never!"

"Look, I hate to waste my time getting some pussy, but if you don't cooperate, I will start carving your lips down there. Oh, that will hurt. If you still don't want to cooperate, well, you see, this knife will take a tour inside that snatch of yours. Oh boy, that won't be a pretty picture, and it definitely won't feel as good as me sliding in my cock. But let's not get ahead of ourselves. We need to take a shower together first. Don't you dare scream! The tip of my knife is right outside...feel it? Oh, I am sorry. I didn't mean to cut some of that beautiful pubic hair. Now slide yourself over while I slide into the shower. No, no, you are forward, and I will be behind you. See, that wasn't so bad."

"Take your hands off me! Don't you dare touch me!"

"Oh, come on bitch! How can I get you wet if I don't squeeze your nipples? Good girl, now bend forward just a little while I slide my cock......."

"HOLD IT RIGHT THERE! DROP THE KNIFE OUT OF THE SHOWER! NOW BACK AWAY FROM HER AND REMOVE YOUR HAND FROM HER BREASTS!"

"Richard! Thank God!" exclaims Julia.

"PUT YOUR HANDS BEHIND YOUR BACK! NOW GET OVER THERE IN THE CORNER! DON'T EVEN TRY ANYTHING. I WILL SHOOT!"

"I am sorry, Julia. Please come here and get this towel. Are you OK? He didn't..?" asks Richard.

"Richard, no he didn't, now please take him to the car and come back in here so we can talk," says Julia.

"Can I have my clothes?" asks Randy.

"Sure, you can put them on in the car, now get going," says Richard.

"Julia, I am so sorry. I didn't mean to..."

"Richard, please stop apologizing. Consider yourself lucky you saw my bare ass earlier, and now you have seen the whole enchilada," says Julia.

"But that wasn't my intention."

"Richard, I am so glad you showed up when you did. If you hadn't, I would have been cut up pretty bad. There was no way he was going to rape me."

"Julia, what do I tell Bobbie? I can't tell her, 'oh, I rescued Julia from being assaulted in the shower by this Charlie/Randy guy and, oh, by the way, I saw Julia in her entire birthday suit; not a stitch of clothes was on her'."

"Richard, tell her what you want, but you won't be able to live with yourself if you don't tell her. After you tell her, just take her to your bed, and she will be OK. You will be too," says Julia.

"Yeah, but remember, Bobbie knows I was falling for you before I finally fell for her."

"So what, Richard? I was married. Where was that going to get you? You really think she will have thoughts that you finally got to see what you fantasied when you had a crush on me?"

"Julia, I never fantasied in seeing you nude."

"Yeah sure, Richard! Drop it! At least you know now how lucky you are to have Bobbie and her young body. Nope, I don't want to hear it, Richard. Remember, I am over ten years older than Bobbie. Now take Randy to the cell and go home to Bobbie and give her your favorite treat," says Julia.

"You know Julia, I thought there was something strange with that Charlie. You know, I once saw a movie with the same thing. This guy pretended to be an innocent little imbecile, and then he switched his personality in the end to the bad guy he really was," says Richard.

"Yeah, I know the movie. I think the character's names were Aaron and Roy," says Julia.

Chapter Fifty-Five

BACK AT THE OFFICE

"Hey guys, how was your extended weekend?" asks Julia. "It was very nice of you to give that to us, Julia," says Bobbie.

"I'll try to do that for you all more often. Before Amanda arrives, I have to discuss something with you, Richard and Bobbie."

"Sure, Julia," says Richard.

"The FBI sent their compensation for our part in stopping the trafficking of under-aged girls. I have a check here for ten thousand dollars made out to the Department," says Julia.

"Wow, they must have felt this was a big deal for us," says Bobbie.

"Yes, I would say so in that Angela and I were almost raped and killed."

"As I heard from Richard, you almost got it the other night. Are you OK, Julia?" asks Bobbie.

"Yes, I am OK. I was a little shaken up at the time, but I feel better now.

"Richard told me all the details. He feels quite guilty!" exclaims Bobbie.

"Bobbie, are you OK with it?"

"Sure, but I warned him that he better see you at all times with clothes on and no fantasizing!"

"Bobbie, I swore to you all of that was in the line of duty. I didn't know Julia was….," says Richard.

"OK, OK, we are over that," says Julia.

"So, what are you going to do with the check, Julia?" asks Bobbie.

"Seeing all of you were involved in pulling this case off, I was thinking of giving you, Richard and Amanda, sixteen hundred each and giving the remaining five thousand to Angela because she was the one who had the most dangerous assignment."

"But what about you, Julia?" asks Richard.

"Well, I am OK. Let me tell you the rest of my idea. I would like to ask Angela to join our team. I would like her to work closely with her sister, and she can help us as well. I would love to see her go to the Academy," says Julia.

"I think that sounds super, Julia! She could use the money for the Academy," says Bobbie.

"The best part is that I can get the City to foot that bill for her. I requested another addition to our team, and they granted it," says Julia.

"This is such a great idea!" exclaims Richard.

"So, you two are good with this? I can present it to Angela?"

"Yes Julia."

"Good morning Amanda and thank you for bringing your sister. How are you, Angela?" asks Julia.

"I am good. Do you think they are really after us?" asks Angela.

"No, not anymore. We cleared that up two nights ago. I will tell you two later, but we are all safe now," says Julia.

"Julia is it OK with you if Angela stays with me and shadows me for today?" asks Amanda.

"Sure, that is why I wanted to talk to you. Let's go into the conference room," says Julia.

Chapter Fifty-Six

THE PROPOSAL

"he FBI gave a very generous amount of money for our part in the case. It all boils down to all of you, Richard, Bobbie, and you Amanda receiving a sixteen-hundred-dollar check. Angela, you will receive a five-thousand-dollar check because you were so instrumental in this case and experienced the most risk."

"Julia, that is way too much," says Amanda.

"Wait a minute. It gets better! Angela, I am offering you a position here, on our team. You can start out helping your sister with her work. I have the authorization to send you, Angela, to the Academy paid by the City. That means the check is yours to do with what you wish."

"Julia, that is so gracious of you!" exclaims Amanda.

"Yes, Julia, I don't know what to say!" exclaims Angela.

"You can start by saying you will accept my invitation."

"Sister, will it be OK if I work with you?"

"Certainly, Angela."

"That means I can be with you all day. I can use the money to pay you for me being able to move in with you," says Angela.

"No, you do not need to pay me. I was going to ask you to move in with me today anyway," says Amanda.

"Julia, why me? Why is it I am so special for you to do this for me?" asks Angela.

"Sweetheart, I feel you and I formed a bond through all of this. Am I right?"

"Yes, I look up to you as an older sister to me besides Amanda," says Angela.

"Julia, is Richard and Bobbie OK with this whole arrangement?" asks Amanda.

"Yes, it has already been discussed with them, and they are excited."

"Hey, new team member, how are you this morning?" asks Richard as he enters the conference room with Bobbie.

"I am great and so thankful for all of you."

"Angela, you earned it!" exclaims Bobbie.

"Angela, look here! This space will be your office," states Julia.

"My own office?" asks Angela.

"Yes, I will have the carpenters in next week to frame it out," says Julia.

"Sis, your first assignment is that stack of papers there on my desk. They need to be sorted and put in the file," says Amanda.

"Where is our receptionist today," asks Bobbie.

"Oh, she is on vacation. We will be accepting the phone calls in her absence," says Julia.

"So, here is our first call for today. I hope it brings us good hope for the community of Harford," says Richard.

Chapter Fifty-Seven

THE PACKAGE

"What is it, Richard? I don't like the look on your face," states Julia.

"It was a call from a Mrs. Rondola. She said she received a package this morning. Her daughter was one of the girls who accepted the invitation to go to Saudi for a career. She was a pole dancer even though she was only fourteen. She said the package contains her daughter's rings and bracelets along with a pair of panties drenched in blood. She is pretty sure it is her daughter's panties. The package is stamped with United States stamps and not overseas," says Richard.

"So, it appears the package was mailed and came from the states. Bobbie, see if you can get Agent Jones on the line. I need to talk to him about this," states Julia.

———

"Yes, sir, OK, we can do that. I will be in touch with you soon," says Julia.

———

"Guys, the FBI is placing this in our laps. They believe this would be a local case and feel we should get started on it. They do not feel it is tied to the trafficking hierarchy, but someone trying to cash in on the situation," says Julia.

"So, we need to find out if what is in the package is authentic to Mrs. Rondola's daughter?" asks Bobbie.

"Yeah, that is where we have to start," says Julia.

ABOUT THE AUTHOR

James Roberts, an emerging author of fictional Crime Thrillers, delivers to his readers the realization of twisted feelings, minds and actions as well as true-to-life situations leading to criminal activities that are sometimes hard to fathom.

This is James Robert's sixth book.